An Amish Holiday Family

Jo Ann Brown

LOVE INSPIRED
INSPIRATIONAL ROMANCE

An Amish Holiday Family

Copyright © 2020 by Jo Ann Ferguson

This edition published by arrangement with Harlequin Books S.A.

For questions and comments about the quality of this book, please contact us at CustomerService@Harlequin.com.

Love Inspired

LOVE INSPIRED
INSPIRATIONAL ROMANCE

LOVE INSPIRED®
INSPIRATIONAL ROMANCE

Recycling programs for this product may not exist in your area.

ISBN-13: 978-1-335-42976-6

An Amish Holiday Family

Copyright © 2020 by Jo Ann Ferguson

This edition published by arrangement with Harlequin Books S.A.

For questions and comments about the quality of this book, please contact us at CustomerService@Harlequin.com.

Love Inspired
22 Adelaide St. West, 40th Floor
Toronto, Ontario M5H 4E3, Canada
www.Harlequin.com

Printed in U.S.A.

For where your treasure is,
there will your heart be also.
—*Matthew* 6:21

For Farah Mullick.
Your smile is as beautiful as your kind heart!
Thanks for loving our books.

Chapter One

Evergreen Corners, Vermont

"What do you think?"

At the deep voice behind her, Beth Ann Overholt almost blurted out the truth. *I don't know what I'm going to do with the rest of my life.* The voice wasn't a familiar one, and she was circumspect, even with friends.

She guessed the man's question hadn't been a personal one, and she realized she was right when he asked, "Do you think it can be rebuilt?"

A ruined covered bridge crossed Washboard Brook in front of her. Part of the span had vanished in last year's flood, leaving only a board or two stretched across the huge arch closer to her. The other half of the arches was hidden within the tilting structure. She couldn't remember if, when she'd been in Evergreen Corners last time, the wooden roof had one side lower than the other. The whole bridge tipped to the left in the direction of the brook's current.

"I wonder," she said as much to herself as the man behind her, "how long it can stand at that angle."

"Not much longer, I'd say."

Beth Ann looked over her shoulder when the man sighed. His face was craggy, as if God had stopped sculpting it partway through, but his deep blue eyes were filled with honest regret. The cold wind blew black hair across his forehead beneath his hat of the same color. Even taller than she was by two or three inches, he wore a dark coat over work-stained broadfall trousers and worn boots.

Was he one of the Amish volunteers who'd come to Evergreen Corners to help rebuild after Hurricanes Kevin and Gail? She didn't recall seeing him before. On her previous visits, she'd spent time painting new houses for families who'd lost everything. This time, she'd only been in the small Vermont town since yesterday.

The man gave her a smile. Though his expression was tinged with sadness, his whole face changed. What had been intimidating became friendly while his eyes glistened with what looked like mischievousness.

"Are you hoping it'll fall in while you're watching?" she asked.

"The opposite. I've been coming out every day or so to make sure it's still standing." He sighed. "I don't know how much longer prayer can keep it from collapsing."

"The village must be—"

"Doing nothing!" His cold voice lashed her like the November wind. "The bridge was damaged during the first hurricane, and the one this year did more harm. Look!" He stretched an arm past her to point at the closer end of the bridge. "See? The abutment is being undermined. If something isn't done soon, the whole bridge will be lost. Where do they think they'll find trees big enough to replace those arches?"

"They'll have to use steel girders."

"What *gut* will that do? A covered bridge sitting on metal arches? It'd be an abomination."

His fervor overwhelmed her, and she wasn't sure how to respond. She understood his admiration for the bridge. Traveling through the covered bridges of Lancaster County had been one of her favorite parts of living there. Many had been washed away by Hurricane Agnes in the 1970s. The replacements had been built to withstand flooding, their steel components hidden behind a wooden facade. Those using the bridges were none the wiser, and tourists still stopped to photograph the barn-red spans.

She doubted the man who'd moved to stand beside her wanted to hear that. He was on a quest to keep the covered bridge as authentic as possible.

So instead of replying to his outburst,

she said, "I'm Elizabeth Overholt, but my friends call me Beth Ann."

His smile rearranged his face again, and she couldn't help being fascinated by how each emotion altered it. "My name's Robert Yoder, and my friends who want to remain my friends don't call me Robbie any longer."

She laughed, surprising herself. "All right... Robert."

"*Gut*, Beth Ann." His smile wavered. "I assume it's okay to call you that."

"It is. Have you been in Evergreen Corners long?"

"About a week. Long enough to get assigned to the team building the final houses. I came to see my sister Rachel and her little girls who live here. When I found out they needed extra hands, I raised mine to volunteer."

"It's impossible not to pitch in when you see how much needs to be done."

"Do you live here?"

She considered telling him she'd come out on the cold day to be by herself and have a chance to think about her future. It seemed bizarre to be asking herself what she wanted to be when she grew up, but she was. However, as she stood by the bridge, her thoughts had been on the past.

About the job she'd already questioned if she wanted to keep before the doctor she'd worked for retired last year, closing the birthing clinic.

About her grandmother's death a month later.

About her attempt to start her own freelance midwifery practice, which had fizzled out because the Amish women she'd assisted had decided to go to an established clinic overseen by a female doctor. It hadn't helped that three women under her previous doctor's care had lost their babies before birth. Each time, Beth Ann had warned the women of the fragility of their pregnancies and urged them to take precautions. Each time, the women had ignored her advice.

She'd heard the whispers. The doctor she'd worked with was too old and she was too young to be a proper midwife, though she was thirty-three.

None of those rumors mattered. What mattered was babies had died. She couldn't imagine losing a child, because she wanted one of her own. She hadn't had any family since her grandmother's death. The grief from that loss remained vivid after a year. Beth Ann barely recalled her parents, who'd died when she was young. Her grandfather had already passed away, so it had been her and Grandmother Overholt.

Her family.

A tiny one in a community where more than the fingers on both hands were often needed to count the members in one household.

She did have a lone living relative. Or at least she thought she did. At last report, her aunt, Helen Friesen, lived in California. She'd moved there before Beth Ann was born and had never come home.

With nothing to hold her to Lancaster County, Beth Ann could go anywhere and do anything she wanted. The problem was she didn't know what she wanted to do. She hoped time working in Evergreen Corners would give her a chance to make decisions about her future.

"No, I don't live in Evergreen Corners," she replied when she realized he was waiting for her answer. "I've come to help whenever I can get away from Pennsylvania. I've become an expert at getting paint out of my hair."

"I don't think there's any painting going on right now," Robert replied.

"That's what I was told when I checked in with Amish Helping Hands yesterday. I'm sure someone will find me something to do pretty soon. I came today to see what happened after this year's hurricane. Once I'm assigned a job, I won't have time for sightseeing." She smiled. "I'm pretty good swinging a hammer." She held up her gloved hands and wiggled her thumbs. "Haven't hit either of these in a long time."

"Well, in that case, you could help me fix the bridge."

She gasped. "You're doing that?"

"I wish I could say *ja*, but it's wishful thinking." He edged closer to the brook's steep bank and stared at the unsteady structure.

"Are you a carpenter?"

"I hope to have my own woodworking shop someday, but for now, I'd like to try to save the bridge."

Beth Ann couldn't dampen her pulse of envy. He sounded as if he knew what he wanted to do with his life for months to come. Months? It might take longer to repair the bridge. During that time, he'd be doing what he wanted to do. How she wished she could feel the same about something!

Something that was possible. What man would want a wife who was in her thirties and wore a brace on her right leg, a reminder of the car accident that had killed her parents when she was four years old? She regretted not spending more time socializing earlier, but she'd learned her lesson when she was dumped by two men in quick succession. Webster Gerig and Ted

Contreras hadn't been very much alike. Webster was tall, thin and outgoing. Ted was shorter and wider and never said two words when one would suffice.

However, they'd been in complete agreement about one matter. Both of them had been attentive until she stood to walk across the room. They'd paled at the sight of her brace. They hadn't dumped her right away or even after tasting her attempts at cooking, a skill she'd never mastered. If they had, maybe her heart wouldn't have been broken so badly. No, both men had waited to end their relationships with her until another woman began to pay attention to them. That had told her she'd been good enough until someone better came along. Though she tried to justify their actions, because who wouldn't prefer a woman who didn't walk with a limp and could cook, she hadn't been able to set aside the hurt and humiliation.

Telling herself she had enough love in her life with her grandmother, she'd spent the next decade focused on her career. For what? Everything was in tatters. Now she couldn't wait more than a few weeks to make up her mind, because her savings wouldn't last forever. She had to figure out by the time the new year arrived what she intended to do with the rest of her life. If only she had some idea what that should be…

"There are a lot of covered bridges in Vermont," she said.

"It would be a shame to lose a single one." He stuck his hands into his coat pockets as another gust of wind warned it was time to head indoors. "I need to talk to whoever is in charge." He looked at her. "Do you know who that would be?"

"Either the mayor or Glen Landis, I'd guess."

"Glen Landis is the project manager who coordinates the work for the aid organizations in Evergreen Corners, ain't so?"

"The Mennonite Disaster Service is here as well as Amish Helping Hands and a few Vermont groups."

"Big job."

She nodded. Like everyone else who'd come to Evergreen Corners to help, she had a lot of respect for Glen. He worked long hours, took no credit for his labor and let others receive the gratitude of the local residents who hadn't known where to turn in the hours after the floodwaters receded.

Glen was another person who knew what he wanted to do and where he belonged. She prayed by working with these dedicated people, inspiration would come and she'd know what to do next.

Robert wasn't sure if Beth Ann started toward the center of the village first or if he did. She'd been kind to listen to him obsess about the bridge. Unlike others, she hadn't told him to focus on the jobs he could do in Evergreen Corners and stop thinking about what might be a lost cause.

His mouth tightened. He couldn't believe the bridge was doomed, and he wasn't about to give up on being part of its reconstruction. He had the skills to bring the bridge back to life. As a boy, he'd sought sanctuary at a nearby house after his *daed* gave him another beating. The elderly man who'd lived there never had asked Robert why he came. Instead Old Terry, as everyone had called him, entertained a wounded little boy with stories of how he'd fixed up the covered bridges on the roads near his farm. Robert had imagined following in the old man's footsteps.

He had his chance if he could figure out how to convince the powers that be in Evergreen Corners to share his passionate desire to see the old bridge repaired. He hadn't thought of Glen Landis, and he appreciated Beth Ann's suggestion.

He glanced at where she walked beside him on the sidewalk that twisted alongside the meandering brook. It was delightful to look a woman level in the eyes. Bright green eyes, Robert noted, the color of the grass in the spring when it first was mowed. They were the perfect complement to her dark brown hair, which glowed red when the sun danced upon what was visible in front of the small *kapp* that identified her as a Mennonite. She wore a black coat with the hem of her dark blue dress beneath it. The fabric was adorned with small white-and-green leaves, but he guessed the style was like what his sisters wore.

After seeing the brace in her right shoe, he kept his gaze from it again. It was a simple plastic device. Held in place by a strip of fabric wrapped around the brace and her shin, it was a garish white against her dark socks.

He wondered why she wore it and if it was temporary or permanent, but didn't want to make her uncomfortable by asking.

"Where are you staying?" Beth Ann asked as they reached the old mill in the heart of the village.

"With other unmarried men in the half-finished apartments in the big barn behind David Riehl's house. There are three apartments in what used to be the loft. We put up wallboard and molding in exchange for a place to stay." He smiled as another gust of icy wind swept past them. "The furnace is functioning. I wouldn't want to sleep in an unheated barn this time of year. How about you?"

"I was given one of the tiny cabins at the Mountain View Motel out past the high school. It's a single room with a kitchenette. It would be cramped with anyone else in there, because there's barely room to turn around." She looked at him, an unsettled expression on her face. "Not that I'm complaining. The space works for me, and I could share it with another volunteer. It's not as if we'll be there much anyhow."

"*Ja*, they keep us busy."

She paused by the crosswalks that marked the center of Evergreen Corners. "I'm sure I'll see you around. At meals if nowhere else."

"Most likely," he said. "*Danki* for listening, Beth Ann."

"I'm glad someone cares about that old bridge. Maybe you'll be the one to make a difference in its future."

"I'd like to think so."

"You convinced me, so you've got a chance of convincing Glen or the mayor."

She smiled. "I'll pray you get the answers you want."

Robert was astonished how her words eased the strictures that had enveloped him the past month. As he watched her walk up the sloping sidewalk, skirting patches of ice, he doubted she could guess how much he appreciated her listening. He'd spent the morning, while working in the next-to-last house being built by the aid organizations, praying God would bring him a solution to save the old bridge.

God had sent Beth Ann Overholt. Not only had she suggested people who might help him, but she'd said the right things to bolster his sagging hopes.

He hadn't expected to find anyone else out by the old bridge on such a cold afternoon. The last two times he'd come to look at it, nobody had been around. Today, he'd planned to scramble onto it and check the inside. A few queries he'd made had revealed nobody had been on the old bridge since a couple of small *kinder* had been found up there.

If he or one of his siblings had tried something so foolhardy, his *daed* would have been furious. None of them wanted to be the target when *Daed* lost his temper because he hadn't held back, leaving them bruised from head to foot.

The Yoder temper.

That's what *Mamm* had called it when *Daed* wasn't near. She'd lamented that it was the burden of every Yoder male and the bane of every other person a Yoder male came into contact with.

He'd hoped the scourge might skip him, but it hadn't. His temper was a hideous beast inside him, waiting for any opportunity to burst out. It frightened him, and he was determined not to pass it along to another generation, which was why he'd remained a bachelor. The decision had cost him several special relationships, but he couldn't commit to a woman. No *kinder* or wife of his should have to fear his temper as he and his siblings had been terrified by their *daed*'s. He'd spent his life trying to control his temper, but to his shame, he sometimes failed. The last time had been more than two years ago when in the blur of red-hot anger he'd spoken the words ending a friendship he treasured.

He must not let that occur again. He needed to focus on that old bridge. If he could convince the authorities in Evergreen Corners to agree to his plan, he'd offer his services to oversee the project. Not as a volunteer, but as a paid contractor. He had to earn money to repay the debts his *daed* had left after his death three weeks ago, and he didn't want to burden his sisters, who had families to raise.

Robert hadn't suspected his *daed* had liked to gamble. He must not have been any *gut* because he owed one hundred thousand dollars to a man who'd come to collect the debt the day after *Daed* was laid to rest.

Robert was grateful he'd convinced the man to give him time to sell the family's farm. He was shocked to discover his *daed* had already sold the land except the two acres where the house and barns stood. A quick offer for the remaining property had been for less than half of what Robert needed to pay off the gambling debts, but he'd accepted, hoping the funds would be enough to gain more time to get the rest. The man his *daed* owed told him the debt must be paid by the first of next June. Almost seven months, but how could he raise more than fifty thousand dollars in less than a year?

He'd come to Evergreen Corners because he hadn't been sure where else to go. Any work available in the village was on a volunteer basis. He could go to a plain community, and someone would offer him room and board in exchange for his help on the farm. That wouldn't give him any income.

In addition, he wanted to spend time with his older sister, who lived in the small town. They'd been apart for twenty years after she'd run away and made an extraordinary life of her own, and he'd felt a hole in his heart every day they'd been separated. If he left Evergreen Corners and returned to the community where he'd lived in Ohio, he wasn't sure when or if they'd ever see each other again.

No, he wouldn't return to Ohio. There, the long shadow of his *daed*'s deeds would smother him. His younger sister had moved the week before *Daed*'s death to Indiana. Maybe he could go there. He hated the idea of working in an RV factory, and he tried not to think how long it would take to pay off his *daed*'s debts while working at minimum wage.

Bowing his head into the wind again, he crossed the street and headed toward his sister's house. He'd pick her brain about how best to deal with Glen and the mayor. Tomorrow, he'd begin his quest to save the bridge. It was the way to save himself from a life of misery for years to come and give him the chance to find a way to submerge his temper. Only then could he try to find his own family to love.

Chapter Two

Beth Ann rubbed her hands against her lower back late the next afternoon as she straightened and looked around the room. She was in the next-to-last house the aid groups had been building in Evergreen Corners. She'd finished taping and mudding the bedroom ceiling. When Michael Miller, who oversaw the project house, had asked if she wanted to do the job, she'd agreed, but now she ached everywhere. She'd spent the whole day stretching to reach the ceiling. She'd been told Robert Yoder would help her, but he hadn't shown up.

She didn't want to think he was another man who'd cut and run after he noticed her brace. If he was, she should be glad she'd found out so quickly.

As she went into the main room to put away the tools she'd been using, she was shocked to discover the team members were talking quietly. Not quietly enough, because she could hear what they said.

"Robert Yoder reamed out the mayor this morning," said a man who'd been working in the kitchen. "I was told you could hear his voice out on the street."

"He said terrible things," added a plain woman named Vera.

"Which is why he got kicked to the curb by the mayor."

"No, that's not what happened," Vera said. "He was asked to leave, but when he didn't, the mayor walked out herself."

"To think an Amish man would…" The *Englischer* scowled. "Sorry, I shouldn't have said that."

Vera patted his arm. "It's okay, Jim. We understand what you meant."

"Good, because I don't." He gave them a

wry grin. "I don't understand any of this. I thought Robert was a good guy."

Beth Ann wanted to assert that Robert had been kind when she'd spoken with him, but didn't. Today was just her second day working with these volunteers. They knew Robert far better than she did. But she couldn't envision him yelling at the mayor. As she listened, she sighed. The only way she was going to know the truth was to ask Robert.

The gossip made her uncomfortable, as it had the first time after her grandmother's death when a baby hadn't survived a birth she attended. The baby had been dead when it emerged, but that didn't stop people from saying she'd dropped the baby or let it suffocate. She'd known the truth, and so had the child's family. Still, the half-truths had hurt. Had that been when she started to question being a midwife? She couldn't be sure.

After cleaning up, Beth Ann headed toward the community center on the other side of the village green. She ignored the snow falling onto the piles from an earlier storm. It was melting as soon as it struck the sidewalk, and the setting sun was trying to peek out from beneath gray banks of clouds.

She'd learned as a midwife not to heed secondhand information. Stories repeated often became rumors with little basis in fact. She'd ask Robert himself what had happened at the mayor's office.

How?

Before she could answer that tough question, she saw a boy standing on the village green, holding his hand out to passersby. He was begging. She frowned as she changed her course to pass close to him.

"Hey, lady," the redheaded boy called as she approached. "Got a buck to help a guy?"

"Aren't you supposed to be in school?" she asked.

"School's out. It's after four. Almost five. Besides, I'm sixteen, so I don't have to go to school anymore."

Her gaze moving up and down the boy

who couldn't be more than twelve was meant to express her disbelief. He was as skinny as an abandoned pup, and his coat didn't close because the zipper was broken. The holes in his jeans weren't because of fashion but because of wear. The fronts of his shoes had been cut away, and his toes extended over the soles.

When she didn't reply, he squirmed and started to walk away.

"If you're hungry," she said to his back, "there's food at the community center."

He looked at her. "That's for the people fixing up the town."

She suspected he'd been sent on his way when he'd gone inside before. The volunteers hadn't recognized the boy was truly hungry. Boys his age were always ready to eat, but she wondered when he'd last had a real meal. Beneath his too-small coat, his collarbones jutted against his skin.

"It's for anyone who needs food and doesn't have a way to cook," she replied.

"I can cook."

"Can you? Maybe you could teach me, because I can't."

"Yeah, right," he sneered. "You're one of those Amish ladies, and you cook up a storm. That's what everyone says."

She didn't argue that she wasn't Amish. She doubted the boy cared. When his stomach growled, shame flashed on his face.

"Look," she said, "it's okay to let others help you."

"I can take care of myself. I'm sixteen."

"I see," she said as he again raised his chin in a pose of defiance.

What she saw was a young boy trying to act as if he were old enough to be treated with the respect due to an adult. Arguing with him about anything would be silly when the child was starving.

"I'm Beth Ann Overholt," she said.

"Douglas."

"Just Douglas?"

"Ain't it enough?"

She didn't react to his attempt to infuriate her with his lack of manners. "I told you my whole name, so I assumed you'd tell me yours."

"You shouldn't assume anything, lady."

"Beth Ann."

"You want me to call you 'Lady Beth Ann'?"

"Beth Ann will do, Douglas Whatever-Your-Last-Name-Is."

"It's Henderson. Okay?" He ground the heel of his holey sneaker into the earth. Or tried to, because the soil was half frozen. "Will you leave me alone so I can get back to what I was doing?"

"Panhandling?"

"What's wrong with hoping folks get some early Christmas cheer by helping those less fortunate?"

"Everything, when you can get all the food you want right there." She pointed across the green to the community center beside the Mennonite chapel.

"*All* the food I want?" He squared his shoulders. "I don't want to be preached at while I'm eating."

"Nobody will preach at you, though you'll

see people thanking God for their food. It never hurts to say thank you, does it?"

"Guess not."

"I'm headed that way. Come and see if what I've told you is true."

"If it isn't?"

She shrugged. "You get out of the cold for a few minutes. That's got to count for something, doesn't it?"

Watching the boy's face, she realized how torn he was between wanting to prove he could fend for himself and his hunger. The need to eat won out, and he went with her toward the community center. He bragged about two dollars an elderly woman had given him.

Inside, the community center was bustling. A few people were already gathered around the mismatched tables, and they were digging into chicken and biscuits. Robert sat alone at the far end, an untouched plate in front of him. He didn't glance up as she and Douglas entered.

One problem at a time. She hung up her coat and waited for the boy to do the same.

She didn't have to urge Douglas to come with her to the kitchen's pass-through window where chicken and gravy bubbled in a slow cooker next to piles of biscuits. Cranberry sauce added to the mouthwatering aroma.

She handed the boy a plate and took one for herself. Going first, because she didn't want to have Douglas be unsure how much he could take, she opened a biscuit and put the two pieces on her plate.

As she spooned gravy and chicken onto the biscuits, she said, "The rule here is take all you want, but eat all you take."

"Uh-huh," he mumbled as he grabbed four biscuits. He poured on so much gravy she thought it would spill off the plate. Somehow, he managed to drop a large blob of cranberry sauce into the middle of the gravy.

"What are those?" he asked, pointing at another tray.

"Bran muffins. The kitchen puts out extras so people can have one with a cup of coffee."

His nose wrinkled. "Ugh! Bran muffins are nasty."

"I think you've got enough food for now." She arched her brows at Abby, the Amish volunteer in charge of the kitchen. Saying nothing, Abby gave her an encouraging smile. Beth Ann was relieved. She'd known the community kitchen wouldn't begrudge a kid a meal, but it was nice nobody was making a big deal of his presence in the community center.

Leading the way to where Robert sat, Beth Ann put down her plate. He frowned, appearing as if the world's weight was upon his shoulders. She wanted to ask him if there were any truth to the rumors about what had happened earlier, but was aware of other ears listening. Most especially, the boy's.

Later, she promised herself.

Robert struggled to hide his curiosity as he looked from Beth Ann to the boy. The rest of the volunteers had avoided him tonight as if he were a leper. Had Beth Ann failed to hear the rumors flying through town as fast as debris from the hurricanes? Another flash of dismay erupted through him. He'd nearly lost his temper that morning.

Hoping his expression didn't reveal his thoughts, he asked, "Who's your friend, Beth Ann?"

She smiled, and he was fascinated by her bright pink cheeks that had been burnished by the wind. Her green eyes didn't match her smile, and he wondered what was bothering her. The boy? No, it must be the tales of Robert's visit with the mayor earlier. Another wave of shame flooded him.

"This is Douglas Henderson," Beth Ann replied with what he could tell was feigned cheerfulness. "Douglas, this is Robert Yoder. He's working in town."

"Nice to meet you, Bob," Douglas said, holding out a small, bony hand.

When Robert took it, the boy shook it hard. Robert arched his brows.

She gave another shrug in answer.

"I go by Robert," he said to the boy.

"La-di-da!"

"Is Robert any fancier than Douglas?" asked Robert.

For once, the boy was shocked into silence. Beth Ann had to look away before Douglas saw her smile. Not that she needed to worry. As she bowed her head to say grace, Douglas dug into his food as if he hadn't eaten in a year.

Robert frowned. The *kind*'s gaunt appearance and ragged clothes shocked him.

He and Beth Ann had finished only half of their meals when the boy bounced to his feet and asked, "Can I have more?"

"Remember what I told you?" she asked.

"Take all you want, but eat all you take." He hesitated before blurting, "I wasn't sure you meant that."

"I try to say what I mean. God asks us to be honest with one another."

"You Amish are so, so weird." He grabbed his plate and rushed to the pass-through window.

Robert shook his head. "Out of the mouths of *bopplin*..."

"Don't let him hear you call him a baby." Pushing aside her half-eaten meal, she asked, "Where were you this afternoon?"

"I'd planned to be there." He wasn't sure what else to say. He couldn't bring himself to tell her how his worst nightmare had come to life when he'd fought to hold on to his temper while in the mayor's office. He might have to explain the rest, including the reason why he couldn't let himself get angry.

How could he explain the truth that shadowed his life? He hadn't told his two sisters about his deepest fear: that Manassas Yoder's volatile temper had been bequeathed to his son. His *daed* had used his hands and belt to punish them. If they'd tried to protect themselves, they were punished more, shut in dark cellars or denied food. The invisible beast within Robert waited, ready to pounce the moment he let his guard down.

It nearly had today.

As if he'd spoken aloud, Beth Ann asked, "What happened between you and the mayor?"

"I should have guessed you'd hear about me going to the mayor's office."

"I've heard several different versions."

He snorted. "I'm not surprised. Folks like to gossip."

"It sounds as if you gave them good reason to." Folding her arms on the table, she watched Douglas take as big a serving as he had the first time. "Did you really yell at Mayor Whittaker?"

He found himself about to tell her everything about how his hopes had been so high when he'd climbed two steps to the town hall. Finding the room number for the mayor's office, he'd known this might be his best—and possibly only—chance to save the covered bridge and his future.

The mayor's office door, her name written in gold letters on the frosted glass, had been ajar. Had it been meant to be an invitation to walk in? Unsure, he'd rapped his knuckles against the wood before he opened it wider.

Gladys Whittaker was seldom seen without her phone pressed to her ear. Sometimes, she held two phones at the same time. However, she'd been focused on paperwork. She'd smiled as he entered, and everything had started out okay.

"I did raise my voice toward the end of our conversation about the covered bridge," Robert admitted. "When I realized what I'd done, I apologized and left." He put his hand on her arm, startling her as much as he did himself. His eyes sought hers across the table. "You believe me, ain't so?"

He could tell his question had stunned her, and he had to wonder why it was so important for her to accept what he said as the truth.

"Of course I do," she replied, and a knot released in the center of his gut. "I was sincere when I said Plain People prefer honesty."

"Which makes us so, so weird." He managed to put the same disdain on the words as Douglas had.

She laughed. "My advice is ignore the gossip. In a small community like this, there will soon be something new to talk about."

Beth Ann added something more, but he didn't hear as he caught sight of Douglas glancing around before reaching out for another handful of food.

When her gaze followed his toward the boy, she gasped. "Oh my! He's stuffing food in his pockets."

"Probably for later."

She shook her head. "I don't think so. He took two bran muffins, and he said he hated bran muffins. I think he's stealing for someone else."

"That's possible."

Standing, she motioned for Robert to come with her. He didn't move.

"We need to talk to him," she insisted.

"You try. You're better with *kinder* than I am."

She gave him a puzzled glance. No doubt, she was wondering why he'd say such a thing, but he knew the truth. He was his *daed*'s son, and he shouldn't be trusted around *kinder.* If he lost his temper as his *daed* had…

Douglas returned to the table. The boy started to sit but paused when she said, "Be careful. You're going to crush those muffins in your pockets."

"Muffins?" He laughed. "I got chicken and biscuits, Lady Beth Ann."

"I saw what you did." She plucked a crumbling muffin from his pocket. Sitting again, she asked, "You don't like these muffins. Who does?"

"I don't know. You want me to ask around?"

She ignored his flippant tone. "Douglas, tell me the truth."

"The truth is it's none of your business."

"You can tell me, or you can explain to the ladies in the kitchen why you're taking the food they made."

He glanced at Robert as if he expected help, then sighed. "Okay. I know someone who's hungry."

"Who?"

"I don't—"

"Give up, Douglas," Robert said with a terse laugh. He shouldn't have been getting involved, but he didn't like watching Beth Ann's attempts at kindness being thrown into her face by a pint-size thief. "You know you might as well tell her, because she's not going to give up until you do."

Panic twisted the child's face. "I ain't done nothing wrong. You said I could take as much as I wanted as long as it got eaten."

"Don't you think," Beth Ann asked, "your friend would like chicken and biscuits and cranberry sauce more than an unbuttered bran muffin?"

"Yeah." The single word was reluctant.

"Finish up your supper while I finish mine. Robert, will you get a take-out box and spoon up a serving of the chicken and biscuits?" She smiled at the boy. "And plenty of cranberry sauce."

"Get two servings," Douglas said in between hasty bites as if he feared she'd take his food off his plate.

Robert nodded and stood.

Beth Ann gave him a swift smile that

danced through his center. He looked away. Leaving the two at the table, he went to ask one of the kitchen ladies for the food. He couldn't stop himself from peeking at the table where Beth Ann watched the boy eat. When Douglas cleaned his plate again, she scraped her own meal onto his. He grunted what might have been gratitude and proceeded to make that food disappear, too.

Robert moved to stand on the boy's side opposite from where Beth Ann stood as they put on their coats, collected two bags of food and headed out into the night. If Douglas tried to run away, one of them was sure to catch him before he got too far. Robert couldn't imagine racing around with such a full stomach, but the boy wasn't happy to be taking them to his friends.

Through a thickening snowstorm, Douglas led them down a street Robert had never been on before. Most of the houses were neatly lit like the rest of the village, but he turned up the walk of the one that wasn't. By the front door, an old claw-foot tub, minus three of its decorative feet, leaned against a stack of rusty metal chairs. An abandoned toilet sat on the other side of the porch next to a pair of refrigerators full of garbage. Even on the cold November night, the stench was appalling.

When the boy climbed the steps, skipping the broken or missing ones, and threaded his way through the junk on the porch, Douglas acted as if he didn't notice the reek. Robert guessed he no longer did.

A curtain moved in the window set into the door, which didn't seem to sit in its jamb. A faint light came from beyond it. When it flickered, Robert realized it must be a candle. Douglas made a quick motion he guessed they weren't supposed to see. Was the *kind* warning someone he wasn't alone?

"Supper's here," Beth Ann called. "Who wants chicken and biscuits?"

The door popped open. Two heads appeared in the light from a candle burning inside what had once been a kerosene lamp. Two redheads who were younger than Douglas. A thin girl and a tiny little boy who dragged his foot as he walked to-ward them.

"You brought us chicken and biscuits, Dougie?" asked the little boy. "It smells good!"

He hooked a thumb behind him. "They've got the food." He aimed a frown at Beth Ann and Robert. "Guess they didn't trust me to carry it."

"We didn't trust you not to eat it," Robert said in a solemn tone that triggered giggles from the younger *kinder*.

Before Douglas could answer, Beth Ann asked, "Will you introduce us?"

Robert thought the boy would refuse, but fatigue was heavy in Douglas's voice as he said, "These two nosy snoops are Robert—don't call him Bob—and Lady Beth Ann. This is Crystal, and the runt is Tommy."

"Ain't a runt," retorted the smaller boy.

"I would say not," Beth Ann hurried to say before an argument could start. "You're a big boy for someone who's..."

"I'm five!" He jutted out his chin in a pose identical to his brother's. "Well, almost five. I'm going to be five on Christmas. Me and Baby Jesus were born on the same day." Without a break to take a breath, he added, "Crystal's eight, and Dougie is twice my age. See? I can do big-boy numbers."

"So I see." Robert was astonished to discover the fast-talking boy was only ten years old.

Looking over their heads, Robert saw paint chipping off the walls and littering the floor in small piles. A single chair was visible, and the seat had half fallen out of it.

"Where do you want to eat?" he asked.

The little boy grasped Beth Ann's hand. "I'll show you!"

Robert tried not to stare at his right foot slapping the floor on every step. His rolling motion was similar to Beth Ann's. Was the little boy supposed to be wearing a brace also?

His attention was pulled away when he heard a moan. Not from the *kinder* or Beth Ann. It came from the house. A warning, if he had to guess, that it needed more than a deep cleaning. The two windows in what he guessed was a dining room were cracked, and their moldings were several degrees off square.

Crystal set the lamp on a table covered with dirty dishes and what looked like rodent droppings.

Putting her hand to her mouth, Beth Ann retched. They couldn't let the *kinder* eat in such conditions.

"Get your coats," he said. "This food has gotten cold. Let's go and get you some warm supper." As the littler ones cheered and ran to get their coats farther in the unlit house, he asked their big brother, "Where are your parents?"

"Our dad is gone." Douglas spoke the words without malice, stating what for him must have been a fact of life. "Mom is in rehab." His mouth twisted. "Again."

"So who lives here with you?"

"Aunt Sharon does."

Robert warned himself to remain calm, but he wanted nothing more than to give the *kinder*'s *aenti* a very large, very angry piece of his mind. The *kinder*'s squalid house was falling down around them. There was no light other than a candle and, from what he could see, no running water. "Can you ask your *aenti* to come and speak to us?"

Crystal came in. "She's not here."

"Where did she go?" Beth Ann asked.

The girl grinned, showing gaps in her teeth where new ones hadn't come in yet. "Las Vegas. She's going to bring me some bling." She paused, looked at her brothers and asked, "What's bling?"

Beth Ann glanced at Robert, and he knew her thoughts matched his. The problem was far bigger than a boy begging and stealing. These youngsters needed an adult in their lives.

He was sure that adult must not be Robert Yoder. As much as he longed for a family of his own, the encounter with the mayor had been a warning. His temper was far from under control, and he didn't want anyone else—not Beth Ann, not the *kinder*—to suffer the next time it overtook him.

Chapter Three

W hen Beth Ann tugged on his arm, drawing Robert away from the *kinder*, he was
amazed he could move when every muscle
seemed frozen. He wasn't sure if he was
more shocked by the state of the house
where the Hendersons lived or by his reaction to Beth Ann's touch. A shimmer of
sensation rippled out from where her fin-
gertips had brushed the bare skin of his
wrist.

Wrong time, his head warned his heart.
The last thing he needed now was to begin
a relationship. He was in debt up to his
ears, and he had no prospects for a job beyond his volunteer work. Worse, he hadn't

learned how to tame the temper he'd inherited from his *daed*.

Beth Ann's mind was on more practical matters, he discovered.

"We've got to help them," she said. "They can't stay here."

"I agree."

She breathed what appeared to be a sigh of relief, and he wondered if she'd expected he'd give her an argument. Anyone with eyes in their head—or a sense of smell—would decide instantly the filthy house was no place for *kinder*.

"Where will they live?" he asked when she remained silent.

"Why not with you?"

"Me?" He recoiled as if she had jumped out at him and shouted, "Boo!" Didn't she realize what she was asking?

No, she didn't. She had no idea how having an instant family, especially one with a boy as rebellious as Douglas Henderson, might become a recipe for the disaster his own youth had been. Already, in the short time since he'd met the boy at the community center, Robert had had to quell his temper when Douglas sassed Beth Ann or showed a total lack of respect for anyone else.

How could he look for a job when he was responsible for three young *kinder*? Maybe when they were in school. Or were they attending school? He didn't know much about *Englisch* education other than it continued beyond the age of fourteen, when formal studies ended for plain scholars.

"Don't you have room for them? You said you're living in David Riehl's barn. It's got to be bigger than the place where I'm staying."

"I've got roommates, and it's under construction. It's no place for *kinder*."

She nodded, unable to argue with those facts. "I don't have much room. Not enough for three children. Could you take the oldest one?"

He noted how careful she was not to speak the boy's name, drawing the *kinder*'s attention. Could he provide shelter for Douglas? It was for a single night. In spite of the warnings shouting in his head, he said, "I'll take him tonight. Tomorrow we need to look at other solutions."

"I agree." She gave him a quick smile. "Thank you, Robert. I don't know where I'd have all of them sleep in my tiny cabin."

He hadn't been sure what he'd say next if she hadn't accepted those facts. He was glad she seemed logical and hadn't pestered him to explain further. Shame swept through him. Being honest meant telling the whole truth, but he couldn't. He didn't know Beth Ann, so he couldn't trust her.

He wanted to laugh. He didn't trust *anyone* with the truth. Not even himself.

"I guess," Beth Ann said, "the first thing is to gather what the children will need tonight. Tomorrow we'll have to alert the authorities that the children were left on their own."

"Why?" When her brows rocketed up, he added, "Sorry. We Amish are accustomed to handling our own problems."

"These children aren't Amish, and neither am I."

Her statement drew him up short. She seemed so much like the plain women he knew he'd let himself forget that important fact.

Before he could speak, she went on, "I know what you're thinking. I seem to know a lot about Amish folk. It's because I've been welcomed into dozens of Amish homes in Lancaster County as their local midwife."

"You're a midwife? How can you get enough time away from your patients to come to Vermont?"

An emotion he couldn't decipher flashed through her eyes. She waved aside his curious questions as if they were unimportant, but he suspected they were as crucial to her as the secret he carried so deep within his heart.

"We can talk about the past later," she replied. "Right now, we need to focus on helping the children."

Not wanting to leave the whole task to her, Robert said, "Let me get what the *kinder* need to take with them."

"All right." Beth Ann hesitated, and he guessed she had no idea where to look in the vile house for what the youngsters needed.

Neither did he.

When he glanced into the dining room, he realized the *kinder* had gotten tired of waiting to eat. They were finishing the meals brought from the community center. He wasn't surprised Douglas had spooned gravy and chicken onto a biscuit for himself. The boy must have a bottomless pit inside him, but he'd waited to assure himself his siblings had enough to eat before he dug in himself.

"Oh, dear," Beth Ann murmured beside him.

He glanced at her. "What's wrong?"

"I'd hoped we could get them out of here before they ate. Who knows how long it's been since those plates were last cleaned?"

"Yummy," announced Tommy. "You make good food, Lady Beth Ann."

"You can call me Beth Ann," she said

with a smile. "I didn't cook that food. The nice ladies at the community center did."

The little boy turned to his big brother. "Can we go there tomorrow to eat?"

Douglas blushed with what Robert guessed was embarrassment, and Beth Ann's laugh startled the boy as much as it did him.

"Yes, you'll be going there tomorrow. At least for breakfast. I eat at the community center, and you can come with me. Hey, I've got an idea." She made it sound as if the thought had just entered her mind. "Come and stay with me tonight. That way, we can go to breakfast together tomorrow. Where I'm staying isn't very big, but it's—"

When she faltered, Robert wondered if she'd been about to say *clean*. Did she think the kids would care about her appraisal of the pigpen where they lived? *Ja*, she did. Her heart must be even gentler than he'd guessed.

"My place has got plenty of room for Crystal and Tommy to have a sleepover with me tonight," she hurried to say. "Douglas, you can stay with the bachelors at Mr. Riehl's barn. We—"

Douglas jumped to his feet. "Get out and don't come back! We don't want your food or your plans or—or—or anything!"

When the boy continued bellowing orders and moved to shove Beth Ann, she caught him by the shoulders before he could knock her off her feet. The other *kinder* cried out in dismay as Douglas squirmed to escape and swung his fists at her, but she held him gently.

"What's wrong?" she asked in little more than a whisper. She repeated the question as if singing a lullaby.

The boy calmed enough to mutter, "We don't need your help."

"I realize that," she replied in the same soft voice. "But we want to help."

"Not my problem."

"If us helping you isn't the problem, what is?"

Before the boy could answer, Crystal got up. She held her younger brother's hand as they walked to Douglas.

"Mommy told us not to let anyone separate us," the girl said with dignity far beyond her age. "We could end up in fester care."

"Yeah," echoed Tommy. "Fester care is the worst."

Beth Ann's mouth twitched, but her voice remained serious. "Have you been in it before?"

"No," Crystal answered, "but Mommy was, and she said our aunt was better than being sucked into the system." Puzzlement clouded her eyes. "Do you know what system she's talking about?"

Robert understood. As a boy, one of his friends had been an *Englischer* living on a nearby farm. The boy had been in foster care. One day, he'd been there, and the next, gone. No explanation as the boy was ripped out of Robert's life. He remembered the boy had spoken of siblings, none of whom he'd seen in years.

"Yes, Crystal, I do," Beth Ann said as he struggled with his memories. "We're talking about tonight only. Douglas can go with Robert, and—"

The *kinder* shook their heads.

Beth Ann sighed. "All right. You all can stay with me tonight. Someone may have to sleep standing up, but we'll figure it out." Without a pause, she added, "In the morning, we'll go to the community center for breakfast. Did you know they've got both pancakes and waffles? So will you come with me tonight?"

Both younger children shot a pleading glance at their big brother. Robert guessed they would have followed Beth Ann to the ends of the earth to get such an enticing breakfast.

"Dougie, let's go with Lady Beth Ann," Crystal urged. "I want pancakes *and* waffles for breakfast."

"Me, too!" piped up Tommy before he reached onto the table for the last biscuit and took a huge bite.

"Douglas?" prompted Beth Ann. "What do you say?"

"We can have both pancakes and waffles?" he asked with suspicion.

"You know the rules at the community center. Take all you want as long as you eat all you take."

"Sounds to me," Robert interjected, "like you can have both pancakes and waffles as well as both bacon and sausage."

As he'd hoped, the mention of bacon and sausage sealed the deal for Douglas. The boy nodded, then halted himself as if he didn't want to show the adults how much he wanted a big breakfast.

Or how much he needed that meal and others. Maybe he was skinny because he was going through a growth spurt. Robert would have liked to believe that, but the stove in the kitchen didn't have a single pot on it. It was an electric stove. How long had the electricity been off in the house? Since their *aenti* left or before?

Beth Ann clapped her hands and said in a cheerful tone, "If you're coming to stay with me, you'll need clothes for tonight and tomorrow."

"What should we bring?" asked Crystal. "Our toothbrushes?"

Beth Ann gave a small shudder. "Why don't we stop at the desk at the motel and pick up new toothbrushes for you? They've got little bars of soap, too, so you can each have your own."

"My own soap?" The girl flung her arms around Beth Ann. "Thank you, Lady Beth Ann."

"Please call me Beth Ann," she replied as she had before, but gave Crystal a squeeze. "You'll need your pajamas and slippers, if you've got them."

"Tommy does, but we don't," Douglas said as he returned to the table and chased the last of the gravy with a final bite of biscuit.

"That's okay. The floors are nice and warm. Of course, you'll need clothes for school tomorrow."

Douglas choked on the biscuit and gravy.

"We don't go to school," Crystal said. "We don't go anywhere. Aunt Sharon told us to stay out of sight."

"I'm sure she'll understand it's okay while you're with me," Beth Ann replied with more serenity than Robert could have dredged out of his outrage at how the *kinder*'s *aenti* had left them on their own.

Tommy's and Crystal's heads moved as one so they could look at their older brother, waiting for his decision. Though none of them had said so, Robert surmised the *kinder* had promised their *aenti* they would do what Douglas told them to do. What a burden for a ten-year-old boy!

Sympathy deepened within Robert when he saw uncertainty and fear in the boy's eyes. Uncertainty about whether he should pass authority for his small family to Beth Ann and fear, no doubt, that if he didn't go along with her, he'd miss out on breakfast.

Again he nodded, but reluctantly.

With a cheer, his brother and sister began to head in two different directions around the table. Beth Ann halted Tommy while Robert called Crystal back. Maybe the *kinder* knew their way around the unlit house, but nobody else did.

Beth Ann asked where their clean clothing was kept. When both pointed to an empty laundry basket, he heard her sigh. However, her smile never wavered when she spoke to the youngsters. She worked with one at a time to get what they'd need for the next few days. They didn't ask why she wanted to have more than a day's supplies, and she didn't explain she was as averse to returning to the house as he was. Whenever she saw the *kinder* about to balk at her requests, she began to talk about the community center kitchen and the treats made there.

He wanted to congratulate her on such a brilliant tactic to keep the kids from thinking about how they were leaving home, but spent his time trying to keep the stacks of clothing—most in need of being laundered—from tipping onto the dirty plates on the table.

When they had enough gathered to satisfy Beth Ann, she asked, "Do you have clean bags?"

Crystal opened one of the filthy kitchen

cabinets and pulled out grocery bags that had been shoved into each other. "Like these?"

"Yes," said Beth Ann.

From where he stood an arm's-length away, he could see what looked like footprints from a mouse across the brown paper. He grabbed a broom leaning against the wall beyond the cupboard where the bags were stored. A faint scrabbling reached his ears, and his stomach turned as he realized the youngsters didn't react to the obvious sound of vermin racing into the shadows.

As she helped Tommy with his tattered coat, he noticed Crystal's was too small and the zipper was broken. Their *mamm* had left their *aenti* in charge, but *Aenti* Sharon was no more capable of taking care of the Henderson *kinder* than their *mamm* was.

Robert picked up the bags, including the one holding trash from tonight's meal. Though dirty dishes remained on the table, he couldn't bring himself to leave the containers they'd brought from the community center. He'd dispose of them later or return them to the kitchen if they were reusable.

"All set?" he called out.

As they walked toward the front door after making sure the candles were out, Tommy let out a wild cry. "I can't leave. Not without Woodsy."

"Who's Woodsy?" Robert asked.

"My bear!" His head swiveled as he looked around. "Where is he?"

Crystal ran into the darkened dining room. He heard a warning creak from the floorboards. How stable was the house? He couldn't miss how the walls bowed.

"Here he is," the girl said when she came back with a stuffed toy. "You put him there while we were playing hide-and-seek, remember?"

As the little boy took the bear that had little of its fur remaining and hugged it close, Robert saw his dismay mirrored on Beth Ann's face. The idea of the *kinder* playing with smelly toys in the filthy house sent shivers of horror along his spine.

He opened the door, desperate to help

the *kinder* flee. After he'd blown out the candle in the lantern and put it outside on the porch, he sucked in great breaths of clean air. He hoped he never encountered the *kinder*'s *mamm* or *aenti*. He feared he wouldn't be able to hold on to his temper and wouldn't be sorry if he lost it.

That thought shook him to the core. It wasn't the way of Plain People to resort to violence to solve their problems or anyone else's, but he was furious at the women who'd abandoned three *kinder*.

The Mountain View Motel had been built, according to the sign by the registration desk, in 1951. It was long and low and snaked along the hillside like a headless dragon. On one side, three small cabins, only a bit larger than the units making up the motel, were clustered near a pair of snow-covered picnic tables.

Beth Ann led the way to the first one, mindful of skirting the snow piles and the freshly fallen inch of snow. None of the children had boots, or so they claimed.

After seeing the state of their clothes and the house, she felt they were being honest. At least, Tommy and Crystal were. Only a fool would believe every word from Douglas's mouth.

She edged around her ancient car. Any hint of a shine had vanished years ago. It seemed to burn more oil than gas, and she hadn't been sure it would get her from Pennsylvania to Vermont. She couldn't afford anything more reliable.

"Here we are," she said with all the cheerfulness she could muster. She set the two bags she carried on the concrete step and pulled out her key. Opening the door, she reached for the light switches. Both the lamp by the door and the interior ceiling light came on. "Welcome to my little home."

She stepped inside, moving two steps until she bumped into the arm of the sofa. The small space held a double bed in an alcove with a bedside table and a lamp. In the living area was the foldout sofa and a table with two chairs. Two taller chairs were shoved beneath the tiny kitchen's counter. A cramped bathroom was behind the other door.

"You live here?"

Shocked Douglas was looking down his nose at her neat and cozy home, she forced a smile. "It's kind of cute."

"If you think so..." His tone seemed too world-weary for his few years.

Or maybe simply weary. She had no idea how long he'd been standing on the village green asking passersby for money.

To Robert, she said, "Thanks for helping with the bags."

"Glad to help." He was appraising the small space with an expression very similar to Douglas's. "Are you going to be okay?"

"We'll be fine." She wished Douglas would reconsider going with Robert to stay in the barn's apartment, but didn't say anything. Upsetting the children again would be silly.

Setting the bag he carried on the bed, Robert beat a hasty retreat after telling her he'd return in the morning. She frowned at the door he closed behind him. Did he dislike all children or just these children? He'd seemed uncomfortable from the moment she had come over the table with Douglas. She didn't have time to ponder those questions, because the children began firing their own in her direction. Where would they sleep? Did she have a TV? How about a bathroom? Was there anything to eat? The last question came, of course, from Douglas.

Turning her attention to the situation at hand, Beth Ann soon had the youngsters sitting with bowls of ice cream. She unpacked the bags and found places for their clothes—most in worse condition than what they were wearing—with the easy efficiency she'd learned from her time in corralling and entertaining children while their mothers were in labor. She supervised baths for the younger two and a shower for Douglas and pulled out the new toothbrushes they'd gotten at the registration desk.

She paused as Crystal and Tommy

jumped onto the bed, each grabbing a pillow. She hadn't decided where everyone would sleep. A quick call to the front desk informed her that, yes, there was a cot she could use, but it couldn't be delivered that night. Trying to imagine where she could squeeze it into the tiny space, she looked at the bed where Douglas sat and chatted with his siblings.

"I'm afraid you'll have to share the bed tonight," she said.

"We don't mind," Crystal replied. "We've been sleeping together lately."

Beth Ann nodded, understanding what the girl didn't say. Without a working furnace, the trio must have cuddled together for warmth. Again she thanked God He'd made sure her path intersected with Douglas's.

"Sorry you got stuck with us." Douglas didn't meet her eyes.

"I'm not stuck with you." She gave the children a warm smile as she motioned for them to climb beneath the covers. "I like having company."

Douglas claimed the side closest to the door. Was he trying to protect his siblings or give himself the chance to be first out of the cabin?

She couldn't guess, and she wasn't going to try. Handing Tommy his stinky teddy bear, she asked, "Shall we say our bedtime prayers together?"

They looked at her as if she'd started speaking an alien language.

"You don't thank God each night for the blessings He brought you today?" She wished she hadn't asked the question when Douglas's eyes narrowed with abrupt anger. The poor child! He hadn't had much to be grateful for, but she hoped that would change.

"Like ice cream?" Tommy asked.

"A bar of soap for myself?" added Crystal.

Happy the younger two had eased the tension, Beth Ann smiled. "Whatever *you* are grateful for is the right thing to thank God for." She bent her head.

She heard stifled giggles when she prayed

aloud about how much she appreciated God letting her meet the Henderson children. She asked if they had anything to add. The younger two added their gratitude for soap and ice cream, but Douglas only grumbled.

"Don't be like that, Dougie. Lady Bee is grateful for us," said Crystal, giving her a new nickname. "The least you can do is be grateful for her."

"I'm grateful for her," said Douglas—or Dougie, as she'd decided she'd call him, too. "Good ole Robert 'don't call me Bob' doesn't like us."

"How can you say that?" Beth Ann asked. "Robert doesn't know you, and you don't know him."

"He acts like we've got cooties," Tommy piped up, not willing to go to sleep if his older brother and sister weren't.

She wanted to retort that Robert didn't act that way, but he'd been quick to find reasons why the Hendersons shouldn't stay in his apartment.

Amish men left raising children to their wives and the other women in the family.

Yet she hadn't ever met one who didn't like children. Most plain men spent time teaching the next generation about the Bible and enjoyed having youngsters tag around behind them so they could learn the skills necessary to be a good member of the community.

She couldn't shake the feeling—which the kids had picked up on, too—that there was more to Robert's discomfort around them.

Tucking the trio in and turning off the lamp by the bed as well as the overhead light, she realized she was going to have to figure out how to have enough light to read in the evening.

She watched as the children surrendered to sleep. She smiled when Crystal shifted so her head was toward the foot of the bed. Dougie gripped his pillow as if he feared it'd fall off. Between them, Tommy clung to the ragged bear.

She could smell the odors the toy's stuffing had picked up from the dirty house. She wondered if the little boy would agree to put his beloved Woodsy in the washing machine.

Or she could put the toy in the bathtub and let Tommy help get his bear clean. After, they'd take the stuffed toy to the dryer in the motel. Tommy could watch his bear tumble inside, something she might convince the little boy was fun for a toy. She'd need to make sure he didn't think it was too much fun and try taking such a ride himself.

She sighed as she pulled out the mattress on the sofa bed, knowing she might as well try to sleep rather than sit in the darkness. She went into the bathroom to change. She took off her brace and set it to one side along with her clothing. She brushed and braided her hair as she did each night. Going into the main room, she discovered she didn't have a blanket, so she pulled the afghan off the couch and wrapped it around herself.

Sleep was elusive, because she kept reliving the events of the so-very-eventful day. Staring at the ceiling that lit up whenever a car or truck passed by on the road, she realized the enormity of the task she'd taken on. What did she know about taking care of someone else's children?

The children were blessed with having one another. Dougie had taken on too much responsibility in the care of his siblings, but she guessed he'd done it because he didn't want them separated. She turned on her side and closed her eyes, praying everything he'd done to help his brother and sister wouldn't be in vain.

Chapter Four

Something disturbed Beth Ann's fitful sleep. She didn't move, but strained her ears, anxious to discover the source of the noise sifting into her dream.

Soft footsteps.

Steady, but uneven footsteps. A step, then a slap. They seemed to be passing right by the foot of her bed.

No, not her bed, she realized as she shifted and an unyielding support cut into her side. She was stretched out on the sleeper couch, which hadn't been designed for comfort.

Keeping the afghan close, she sat. Squinting into the dark, she tried to see who was walking past her bed. As good sense emerged out of her sleep, she realized she must have heard one of the children going to or from the bathroom. She'd been living on her own for too long.

She settled into her pillow, hoping for sleep to return. It had begun to cover her like a warm blanket when another sound brought her to her feet.

A frightened cry came out of the dark.

And into her heart.

Without her brace, her steps were uneven as she rushed into the bathroom. She knew, without turning on the light, who stood by the tub because what she'd heard must have been Tommy's footsteps.

In the moonlight, she could see the little boy had his arms wrapped around himself as he crouched on the floor. She dropped to her knees and enfolded him against her. She didn't speak, unsure if he was awake or walking in his sleep.

"Lady Bee?" Incredulity filled his voice.

"Sweetheart, you can call me Beth Ann. You don't need to use *lady*."

He shook his head, his hair brushing her cheek. "I'm scared."

"I know, sweetheart." She ran her hand up and down his back in a slow rhythm she hoped his breathing would match.

"Where are we?"

"At my cabin. Remember? You came with your sister and brother to spend the night with me."

He nodded. "I'm scared."

"Would you like to sleep with me tonight?" She released him and clenched her fists and flexed her muscles as if she were a superhero. "I've been known to scare off nightmares."

"All right." He remained serious, but at least he took her hand as she came to her feet. He shook his head when she asked if he needed to use the bathroom.

As they walked into the other room, she couldn't help noting how their footfalls matched. Tomorrow, she'd ask if he had a brace to wear to help his gait. Even if he hated it, as she had hers when she was a child, she knew how important it was for him to use it.

As he nestled into the foldout, pressing to her like a puppy to its mother, she closed her eyes. She was a light sleeper, so she doubted she'd get more tonight. Feeling the soft coolness of his breath against her nape as he began to snore, she tried to shift away from him to give them both a bit more room. His arm reached out and settled on her shoulder. A moment later, he was close to her once more.

She looked over her shoulder. Tommy was asleep, but his brow was threaded with lines of worry.

Her heart ached. Three children left to fend for themselves.

A soft whimpering in her ear broke her heart anew. She put her hand on Tommy's draped atop her shoulder. When his fingers clutched hers, she knew one night's sleep wasn't too much of a sacrifice to let the little boy find peace.

Since the first hurricane more than a year ago, Elton Hershey, the local Mennonite pastor, had handled plenty of problems.

Beth Ann had to wonder if he'd faced any like the dilemma she and Robert brought to him before breakfast the next morning.

The three of them were in the pastor's cluttered office while the children sat out in the hall. The pastor's assistant watched them eat the lollipops she'd found somewhere behind the counter. Beth Ann didn't worry about the candy ruining the kids' appetites. Nothing could. They'd finished off everything in her tiny refrigerator last night and emptied out the few boxes in her cupboard this morning as soon as they woke. While they'd had cereal and toast, they hadn't spoken of anything but how many pancakes and waffles they planned to devour.

"We had no idea the children had been left alone and their living conditions were so awful," Pastor Hershey said, ignoring his cell phone as it rang. From outside the office, a landline began demanding attention, but he kept his gaze on Beth Ann and Robert.

"We aren't looking to blame anyone," Robert said.

Robert had returned, as he'd said he would, to help Beth Ann get the kids to breakfast. When she'd opened the door to find him on the other side, she was delighted to see the cot he'd brought with him. The reception desk clerk had seen him coming up the street and asked if he'd deliver it to Beth Ann's cabin. While Robert set up the cot, Beth Ann kept the children from "helping," turning a quick job into one taking twice as long.

"That's right," Beth Ann said when the pastor folded his arms on top of his desk. "We want to make sure the children are cared for. We figured you'd be able to advise us which agency we need to contact to get help."

Pastor Hershey, a man in his forties with a receding hairline and gentle brown eyes, nodded. "The Vermont Department for Children and Families is whom we should call. They'll find the children a foster home, and—"

"Together?"

He shook his head. "There aren't a lot of families who could take three children on such short notice."

"The children won't be separated," she said, leaning forward. They needed Pastor Hershey's help, but he had to comprehend how the children were determined to remain together...no matter what. "Their mother was in what they call 'fester care,' and they're terrified of it. If you could see the place they were living in an effort to maintain what family they had left, you'd understand."

"I can guess." Pastor Hershey ran his hand across his broad forehead. "Kim Henderson, their mother, has been fighting an opioid addiction for six years."

"Their father?"

"He died of an overdose the week before Tommy's birth."

"That's tragic." The weight of tears pressed against her eyes. She hadn't realized how much she'd hoped there was another parent somewhere who could take the children.

"It is." Pastor Hershey opened a drawer and pulled out what looked like a directory. "It's a tale that's been repeated too often." Opening the book, he said, "I've got a friend at DCF, and he might be willing to grant temporary custody to someone I recommend. Just through the holidays, mind you."

Robert said, "I think that would be easier for the *kinder* than separating them. I suspect Dougie will run away to try to find his sister and brother."

"Robert's right," Beth Ann added. "Dougie feels responsible for them, and he's not going to relinquish that job to anyone."

"So you'd be willing to take temporary custody of the children, Beth Ann?" asked the pastor.

"Me?" she squeaked. Didn't he have a family in his congregation in mind to serve as temporary guardians for the children?

"Would you if it's possible?" He arched one brow. "I'm not saying it is, but my friend focuses on the best interests of children. It would help if I can say someone's willing to oversee the children until Christmas."

Beth Ann looked from his earnest face to Robert's astonished one and at her hands clasped in her lap. *God*, she prayed, *I know I've been praying for guidance about what to do with my life. If this is Your plan for me, I'll do my best to follow it. But isn't there someone better to take care of these children?*

As if in answer, she heard a voice from her memory. Her grandmother's voice, urging her to think of how she could serve others. *Beth Ann, a midwife's job doesn't end with a birth. We serve the whole community throughout every day—and every night—of our lives. Where there is need and where we can help in any way—no matter how big or small—we must be there.*

Raising her head, she said, "I'd be willing, but where I'm living is teeny."

"I'm sure we can find somewhere else for you to live. Many volunteers have left recently because most of the work is done." He smiled and gave a deep chuckle. "I can see what you're thinking. If there are empty apartments, why were you put in that little cabin? The owner has been eager to help the town, and we didn't want to hurt his feelings. Would you agree to oversee the children through the holidays, Beth Ann?" He pursed his lips. "I'll be blunt. Most folks in town have made up their minds about the Hendersons, and those opinions aren't good. I'm pleased you are more openhearted." He got up. "Take the kids to breakfast while I make a few calls."

Beth Ann argued, "We need to get some things from their house, and—"

"Don't go in there until we learn what DCF intends to do." He gave them a sad smile. "It's stood this long, so I suspect it'll be there by the time we've got answers. I'll let you know what I hear as soon as I do."

Beth Ann somehow got her feet under her and stood. Her head was reeling. It'd been the right thing to offer to take the children, but what did she know about being a mother of three children who closed ranks without warning? She prayed she was doing the right thing for them.

Robert followed Beth Ann out of the pastor's office. They collected the *kinder* to the relief of the pastor's assistant, who'd done everything she could to keep them entertained. Like a row of ducklings, the *kinder* followed Beth Ann and him to where the meal was being served. He thought they wouldn't listen to her when she insisted they hang up their coats before getting in line for food. They never took their gazes from the bounty.

While she helped Crystal and Tommy fill their plates, making sure they didn't take so much food that it fell on the floor, Robert supervised Dougie. He reminded the boy—yet again—he could have more as long as he ate it. From what he'd seen, eating all the food wouldn't be a problem for Dougie.

It was his and Beth Ann's turn to go and get food. He watched her try in vain to stifle a yawn.

"Tommy slept well last night on the fold-out, but I didn't," she said with another yawn.

"The cot should help."

"He had a nightmare, and he wanted someone to comfort him." Tears filled her eyes, turning them bright green. "I'm sorry. Every time I think of those children in that horrible house..."

He handed her a plate, flustered by her open emotion. He was also a bit envious she could be so candid when he had to guard every reaction inside him. "They aren't going back there." Robert added scrambled eggs to his plate. "Nobody is until we're given permission from the state. When Pastor Hershey asked if you'd take the *kinder*, I wasn't sure if you'd agree."

"It's a short time. You would have done the same thing if he'd asked you."

He didn't answer, and she looked at him in astonishment. He averted his gaze. Heat rose up his neck, and he hoped he wasn't flushing.

Though she clearly was curious what was

wrong, to his relief, she asked, "If the children come to live with me, will you help me?"

"As much as I can."

He saw she wasn't fooled. Most days, he would be busy at the project house, and he wanted to work on the old covered bridge. In addition, his sister and her family lived in Evergreen Corners. That wouldn't leave him time for anything else.

"Where are you headed after breakfast?" she asked.

"I thought I'd talk to Glen—"

"He's out of town today. Something about closing down the projects after we finish the final houses."

"If that's the case, I guess I'll head to the work site."

She hesitated as he picked up silverware from the tray. "Robert, could you skip work this morning?"

"Why?" he asked as they walked to where the children were eating with great enthusiasm.

"I could use your help."

"With?"

"Something important." She stopped and lowered her voice. "They need something decent to wear to school. I thought I'd take them shopping."

"That's going to be expensive."

"I've got savings, and I'm sure others will be willing to help."

He gave her a quick smile. "After seeing the work the volunteers have done, I don't have any doubts. I can give—"

"I'd rather have your time than your money."

"What do you mean?"

"Dougie would appreciate your help more than mine."

"I don't know how much help I'll be."

"Keeping track of them in a store isn't going to be easy. I could use another set of adult eyes."

His gaze slid away. "All right, assuming it's okay with Pastor Hershey."

Realizing she was pleased, he couldn't keep from smiling as he followed her to the table. He sat when she did and bowed his head to thank God for the meal. It was his last quiet moment during breakfast. He took about two bites of pancake before Tommy wanted his help to get more.

Seconds after Beth Ann was called away to speak with Pastor Hershey, Crystal needed help. As he held the girl's plate steady while she deliberated over the exact banana and orange she wanted, he kept glancing between the two speaking by the door and the boys at the table. He wanted to excuse himself and go to listen to what the minister had learned from his friend, but Tommy spilled his milk down the front of him and needed to be cleaned up.

By the time he and the little boy had returned from the bathroom, Robert's stomach was growling. He hadn't had more than two bites and not a single sip of *kaffi*.

Beth Ann pointed at his cup. "I warmed it up for you."

"Danki." He wanted to ask what Pastor Hershey had found out, but wasn't sure if she'd feel comfortable talking about it in front of the *kinder*.

Beth Ann took a bite of her toast, then reached for blueberry jam in a bowl on the table. "I was thinking," she said as if what she was about to say were of little consequence, "my cabin is way too small."

"It's big enough. Nobody had to sleep standing up." Dougie spoke around a mouthful of food, but she didn't chide him.

Robert guessed it would have been a waste of breath.

"Pastor Hershey has found me a nice place to stay," she answered. "In an apartment over a garage where I could keep my car so I don't have to brush off snow after each storm."

"You've got a car?" Robert asked at the same time Dougie did.

"How do you think I got from Pennsylvania?" She smiled. "My church district allows our members to have cars as long as any chrome is covered over with black paint. That's never been an issue with my beat-up old car. However, the important thing is the nice, big apartment, where Isaac Kauffman has been living with his sister Abby, is going to be vacant by the end of the week."

"Can we help?" asked Crystal.

"Of course you can." Her smile was aimed at each of them, one at a time, around the table.

Robert wondered if the *kinder* felt the same warmth he did when that sweet expression was focused on them. In the brief time he'd known her, he'd learned no one else had a smile like Beth Ann's.

"We'll order pizza," she said. "Pastor Hershey tells me it's the usual food when someone moves from one place to another."

As the *kinder* began to discuss which toppings they'd have, Robert lowered his voice to ask, "Where are the Kauffmans going?"

"Abby will be staying with the Millers, and Isaac is going to become your roommate. Pastor Hershey said one of the guys is leaving to go home."

Robert nodded. "That's right. Vince is heading to Ohio because his brother is getting married."

"Pastor Hershey told me the house where

the children were living has been condemned, so nobody can go in it. That's when he asked Gladys Whittaker if the children and I could move into the apartment next to her house."

"The apartment belongs to the mayor?" A frisson of hope burst out of what he had thought was a dead issue. If the *kinder* were living so close to the mayor, he'd have the excuse he needed to present his case for the covered bridge's reconstruction to Mayor Whittaker in a calm manner. He wouldn't have to sound so desperate and get upset when she spoke about budgets and priorities. With enough money to last him until February or March, if he was frugal, he could take his time and persuade her to his point of view.

"Yes," Beth Ann replied. "The apartment has two bedrooms and a living room and a full kitchen as well as a table with enough room for us."

"And a place for your car? I didn't know you had one."

"Like I said, my church allows them.

When I needed to get to assist in a birth in the middle of the night, it was far better than a buggy. The local Amish knew I was familiar enough with their *Ordnungs* so I was welcomed into their homes."

He should have realized she'd spent enough time with the Amish to be familiar with how an *Ordnung*, the rules by which a community lived, could vary from one district to another. He was pleased she felt comfortable with the Amish.

Because she's part of your life now, his brain answered.

Because she's someone special, his heart added.

Robert tried not to heed either small voice while he ate his cold breakfast and sipped his hot *kaffi*. He listened as Beth Ann talked to the *kinder* about staying with her at the new apartment and taking them shopping for new clothes. Amazed at how she led them to believe each was their own idea, he knew he could learn from her gentle methods and use them when speaking with

Mayor Whittaker or Glen Landis about the covered bridge.

Finally the *kinder* couldn't eat more, and Beth Ann had Tommy and Crystal collect the used plates and silverware. She asked Dougie to take the piles to the tubs filled with soapy water where they'd be gathered and washed in the kitchen. The youngsters complied while he downed the last of his *kaffi*.

Getting up, Beth Ann hesitated. "I'd assumed I'd take the kids in the car, but I don't have a child booster seat for Tommy. How am I going to tell them I can't take them today? I don't want them to go to school in rags."

"I've got an idea." When she looked at him with an unspoken question, he said, "I'll be back in about fifteen minutes."

"What—?"

"You'll see." He rushed away before she could pose another question.

Grabbing his coat and hat, he loped out of the building and down the street, watching out for ice on the sidewalk. He wanted to help where he could, and he thought he knew the way to do that.

Robert was back in less than ten minutes. It'd taken Beth Ann that long to get the kids into their outer clothing while trying to answer questions from other volunteers. More than once, she shook her head and glanced at the Hendersons, making it clear the answer to a question would have led in a direction she didn't want to go when they could overhear. The others respected her discretion, but she could see their open curiosity about the children's situation.

Pastor Hershey had returned and volunteered to share the news about the children. She'd accepted his offer with relief. She needed to think about getting the children outfitted in decent clothing and moving to the new apartment. The thought of the challenges ahead of her daunted her, but God had led her to this, and she was as determined to do His will as the kids were to stay together. Somehow, they'd make it work.

Hearing a shout from outside, she looked

up from buttoning her coat to see a man she didn't know pointing out the door.

The kids ran to see what was going on, and she gave chase. They bumped into one another in front of the community center as a gray-topped buggy came toward them.

Robert drew in the reins. Holding the excited children so they didn't make a sudden move and spook the horse, Beth Ann smiled.

Why hadn't she considered a buggy would be the perfect answer to her dilemma? Booster seats weren't required in a buggy.

"What a good idea!" she called as she took Tommy and Crystal by the hand and followed an excited Dougie onto the sidewalk.

"This is the second buggy in Evergreen Corners," Robert said as he climbed out. "It was delivered last week. The first one arrived the week before. The Millers have it, but this one belongs to my sister and..."

Beth Ann understood what he didn't say. The buggy belonged to his sister Rachel and her future husband. Though Amish claimed they never spoke about a pending betrothal before plans to wed were published, she'd heard Rachel, who was a widow, intended to marry Isaac Kauffman as soon as she was baptized.

When she didn't speak, he gave her a grateful glance before saying, "It belongs to my sister."

"What's the horsey's name?" asked Tommy.

"Clipper. My sister warned me it's because he's been known to like to stretch out his legs on an outing. He'll make the trip to the store in no time flat."

Dougie gasped. "We're riding in *that* fancy carriage?" He rocked from one foot to the other, looking as young as his little brother. "Can I drive?"

She smiled. "It's not fancy, and it's not a carriage. It's a buggy, and it's considered plain like everything Amish folks own."

"It's got pretty seats," argued Crystal as she stretched out her fingers to run them along the dark blue upholstery. "It feels like a cat."

"The seats are made to be durable and easy to clean." She took the younger children again by the hand and led them around to the back. Unhooking the gray canvas flap, she started to lift it.

"Let me," Robert said as he took the uncooperative fabric from her and raised it enough so she could lift Tommy over the rear seat.

Beth Ann cupped her hands and gave Crystal a leg up to climb in after her younger brother. She turned to do the same for Dougie, but he disdained her help and, grabbing the seat, scrambled up on his own.

The older boy frowned. "Hey, this isn't where the driver sits."

"No, it isn't." Robert dropped the canvas. When Beth Ann motioned she'd tie it into place, he went around to the side and climbed into the front seat. As she took a seat beside him, he looked over his shoulder. "A horse is like a car. You can't drive it without lessons."

"Will you teach me?" Dougie asked.

"Me, too," echoed his siblings as he gave Clipper the order to go.

"You're too young yet," Robert said.

"When did *you* learn to drive?" Dougie rested his arms on the front seat.

"When I was…" He gulped.

"Most plain boys learn to drive," she said, "around eleven or so."

"I'll be eleven in February," the boy replied. "Will you teach me?"

Beth Ann couldn't keep from laughing at the shock on Robert's face. "It looks as if you're about to become a driving teacher."

"I guess I am." He turned to look at her as Dougie began regaling his siblings with stories about how life would be once he learned to drive a buggy. Beneath the excited voices from the back seat, he asked, "How about you?"

"How about me what?"

"Do you know how to drive a buggy?"

"No."

He gave her a grin. "I'd say it's time you

learned, too. It'll be a *gut* way for me to practice being a teacher."

"So I'll be your guinea pig?"

"Something like that." When he chuckled, she joined in. She had to admit she liked the idea of spending more time with Robert, knowing they never could be more than friends because he was Amish and she wasn't. He wouldn't look at her as a possible wife and then turn away because of the brace she wore.

For now, that would be for the best. Wouldn't it?

Chapter Five

❧

When Robert looked back on the following three days, he wasn't sure how they survived the chaos. The shopping trip ended with the buggy filled with enough bags so each of the *kinder* had clothing for several days. Knowing Beth Ann was grateful there was a tiny laundry room attached to the mayor's garage, he guessed she'd be doing wash every day. Tommy didn't seem able to get through a meal without spilling something on himself and, often, someone else. She'd insisted on everything being able to be washed and dried. Even their new winter coats and sneakers could go into the washer.

He'd spent the past three days working at the project house during the day and trying to spend time with the *kinder* in the evening, so Beth Ann could have time for laundry or mending holes in the kids' older clothes. She was exhausted and frustrated, and so was he, but not with the demands of her new family.

He was frustrated because it seemed each time he'd needed a tool at the project house, it had been missing from where it should be stored. Others had begun to complain about tools not being where they'd left them. When Michael had brought everyone together for a meeting, they realized it might not have been negligence on the part of their harried team.

Tools weren't misplaced. They were gone.

Was someone helping themselves to the tools? Michael had cautioned them not to start looking at one another as potential thieves. There might be another explanation, and they needed to continue to work together. Robert appreciated Michael's caution, but he sensed their leader thought a thief had been sneaking into the house.

Robert did, too, but he didn't know anyone in Evergreen Corners well enough to guess who might be behind the vanished tools. He'd been relieved when Beth Ann asked for his help with the move. It was an excuse to avoid the strained work site for a day.

Beth Ann and the Henderson *kinder* settled into the apartment over Gladys Whittaker's garage as soon as the Kauffmans had vacated it. The space was about twice the size of the cabin where they'd been squeezed in together. The tiny living room had a foldout couch that Dougie claimed. Robert hoped Dougie wasn't planning to slip out during the night, but doubted he'd leave his siblings even for a short time.

With the bed open, there wasn't room for the dining table. Robert brought a smaller table he'd been working on in the unfinished apartment next to where he was living.

When Beth Ann saw it, she stared. "This is beautiful. Where did it come from?"

"I built it."

"You do fine woodworking, Robert."

He was about to explain how he'd found a haven in working with Old Terry, but one of the *kinder* called for her to come into the larger bedroom where the two younger ones would sleep. He smiled as she rushed away to answer them.

The bunk beds delighted both Crystal and Tommy, though there was debate about who would sleep where until Tommy climbed to the top and decided he'd preferred the bottom bunk. The bathroom had a shower, which thrilled the kids. In Beth Ann's room were a comfortable bed and a dresser and a tiny closet. The kitchen was barely larger than the one at the cabin.

It seemed like a place that could become home, and Robert was surprised at his pinch of envy. Since he'd sold the remnants of his family's farm, he'd felt lost. His hopes that he'd regain his roots in Evergreen Corners, because his sister and her family lived there, hadn't come to fruition. *Not yet*, he'd remind himself, cautioning patience. Rachel had confided she was beginning to feel like she was a true resident of the small town, and she'd lived there for several months.

Putting the last bag from the cabin on the floor next to the packed boxes and bags and Beth Ann's single battered suitcase, Robert was amazed when Tommy grabbed his hand.

"C'mere," the little boy said. "See my new bed."

Robert glanced toward the kitchen where Beth Ann was unpacking the groceries she'd brought. Seeing the small stack of boxes and cans, he wondered how long it would take the state to send its first stipend for the *kinder*'s upkeep. Pastor Hershey had offered Beth Ann money from the chapel's coffers, which she'd accepted, but with more storage space, she needed plenty of money to fill her cupboards and three ravenous *kinder*.

"Go ahead," she said with a smile. "He can't wait to show it off to someone."

"Let me know if you need anything."

"Don't worry," said Dougie as he dumped clothes on the sofa. "We will."

The boy was, Robert guessed, hiding uneasiness behind an abrasive attitude. The youngsters had lost their *mamm*, had their *aenti* abandon them and moved in with Beth Ann and now into the apartment. Giving the kids some slack would be wise. He wouldn't let Dougie's sarcastic comments get under his skin.

"Are you coming?" demanded Tommy, his hands fisted on his hips.

"Right behind you," Robert answered.

This morning, as they began carrying the boxes and bags across the village green, Beth Ann had urged him to be himself around the Henderson *kinder*. She wouldn't have if she'd had any idea what his childhood had been like. He'd seldom experienced any interactions with his *daed* that didn't end with a slap across the face or worse.

After admiring Tommy's new bed and agreeing Woodsy, his stuffed bear, looked very much at home on the lower bunk, Robert went into the living room and opened a heavy box.

It was, as he'd guessed, filled with books Beth Ann had brought with her from Pennsylvania. He saw romance novels and a few mysteries as well as a daily devotional and a well-thumbed Bible.

"Those go on the top of the dresser in the bedroom," Beth Ann said behind him. Frowning, she reached past him and picked up a small box on the window sill. "What's this?"

"Something I thought you might enjoy."

Her eyes widened when she looked at the box with its photo of a tiny lamp with a clip at the end. It would hook onto a book or a piece of furniture, and according to the information printed on the box, its thin stream of light would make it possible for her to read without waking the children.

"What a clever device!" she exclaimed.

"I saw it when I was looking around the store in town the other day, and I thought you should have it."

"How much do I owe you?"

"You owe me?" He gave a quick laugh. "I owe you for taking the lion's share of the care of the *kinder*. Getting you this little light hardly pays you back."

"I didn't know we were keeping score."

"We aren't." He grimaced. "Can't you accept it as a gift?"

"Of course I can." She looked chagrined. "I'm sorry, Robert. I should have thanked you."

He thought of different things to say, things like he appreciated how she hadn't complained he'd spent more time working than with her and the *kinder*. How he'd been glad to spend some of his dwindling funds to buy her the gift. How he wished they could have another chance to speak as they had by the covered bridge before the *kinder* had burst into their lives and kept her so busy.

Instead he said, "I should have understood how you might question why a stranger bought you a gift."

"Stranger? Do you think that's what I consider you?" She laughed. "After the past week, I'd say we've deserved the right to call each other friend."

"I agree." He turned away as if interested in the box. He hoped his face didn't reveal how pleasing her words were, because talking about being friends led him to think about spending more time with her. That must not happen. Even if she were Amish, he had nothing to offer her. Not when his pockets were almost empty, and he had no prospects for the future.

Monday morning was chaos. Beth Ann was pulled one way and another by questions from the children as she helped them get ready for school. Yesterday, when she'd taken them to church with her, hadn't been so hectic. The kids had been curious about the service, and they'd sat without fidgeting while Pastor Hershey gave his sermon. They'd smiled when older members of the congregation smiled and patted their heads.

Yesterday's good behavior was gone. Dougie wasn't happy about going to school while Crystal and Tommy couldn't contain their excitement. That meant another change of clothing for the little boy because he spilled his milk *and* his orange juice during breakfast.

She glanced at the clock, hoping the children weren't going to be late. School started at eight, and it would take five minutes for her to go across the green and up the street.

"I want penders," Tommy demanded with a pout when she put out a dry shirt and pants on the bed for him.

"Penders?" she repeated.

He nodded. "Penders!"

She looked at Crystal, who stood in the doorway. The girl sometimes could translate what her little brother meant, but she shrugged.

"Let's talk about it after school," Beth Ann said with a smile. "How's that?"

Tommy's pout eased, but she could tell he wasn't happy about delaying any discussion about penders…whatever they were.

When she heard a knock on the door, she wanted to groan with frustration. Who was coming to the apartment at this time of day on a Monday morning?

Beth Ann rushed out as Dougie opened the door. She halted in mid-step when she saw Robert at the top of the stairs.

"I thought you might need help," he said.

Her first impulse was to give him a big kiss on the cheek, but she quelled it. First, because it would embarrass him. Second, because she wasn't sure if she'd be satisfied with kissing just his cheek. The thought unsettled her, and she found herself stumbling for words.

She settled for, "Thanks, Robert. Come in."

Crystal and Dougie asked her a question about lunch at the same time. Assuring them Pastor Hershey had made arrangements so they could eat in the cafeteria, she hoped the questions didn't mean there had been days when, without money to pay and too much pride to ask, they hadn't gotten anything to eat.

Making sure they had the right backpack, because Dougie and Tommy had chosen identical ones with their favorite superhero, she pulled on her coat. She bent to help Tommy with his zipper, but kept an eye on the older two. Dougie thought he was too old to wear his coat, and Crystal copied what he did.

Robert picked up a stack of papers she'd left on the table so she'd remember to take them with her. Flipping through them, he frowned. "Why isn't my name on this?"

She'd assumed he wouldn't want to be an emergency contact for the children. As she took the stapled pages from him, she said, "You don't have a cell phone or an answering machine where you're staying, so how would they contact you? I thought it would be better to have Pastor Hershey's office on the form because there's someone there during the day."

"I didn't mean that section. What about this section?" He pointed to the list of names of who could pick up the children. "Why isn't my name on it?"

"I wasn't sure you'd want to be."

He blinked once, then twice.

"If you want," she said, "you can come with us and have your name added."

"I can put my name on here."

"They'll want to meet you first. With most parents, the school office asks for a photo ID and takes a photo, so it can be matched when someone asks to pick up a child." She raised her hand before he could protest. "I know you won't want to have your picture taken, Robert. So that's why you're going to have to go in person."

"Paperwork is the same the world around, ain't so?"

She smiled at the teasing question as she motioned for the kids to go outside. Grabbing her black purse and buttoning her own coat, she waited until Robert had followed them before she closed the door behind her.

She took Tommy's hand as they descended the stairs. Robert offered his to Crystal, but the girl must not have seen it, because she skipped down on her own, trying to keep up with her big brother. When Robert cautioned them not to cross the street on their own, both kids shot him a peeved frown.

"He's right," Beth Ann said, though the kids had wandered around town without adult guidance since their aunt had left them.

She ignored their grumbling and held the younger children's hands as they crossed to the village green. Releasing them, she smiled as they chased after Dougie, who sprinted through the snow.

As Robert matched her steps, he said, "They aren't comfortable around me."

"Because you aren't comfortable around them."

Her words pricked him because his shoulders stiffened. "I didn't know it was obvious."

"Kids see things more clearly than adults do. Maybe it's because they're dependent on us, but they watch for signals to guess what we're thinking." She patted his arm. "Be yourself around them."

"Be myself?" He arched his brows, but

she couldn't guess why he seemed to think that wasn't a good idea.

She didn't ask while they walked to the elementary school. The original building had been destroyed during the floods. Classes were in portable classrooms set to the far side of the playground while work was being completed on the replacement building. The cluster of trailers provided space for kindergarten through fourth grade, and the middle school pupils were being taught in what had been the Grange Hall. A single battered tree stood in the yard. The scarred earth was hidden beneath snow that also covered the top of a metal box where donations could be left for the plantings fund.

The building holding the administrative offices was set to one side. Along the walls of the hall was artwork by the students. A table held a half dozen resin turkeys flanked by straw cornucopias.

"The office is to the left, right?" Beth Ann asked.

"Left or right?" asked Tommy, looking in both directions.

She smiled. "I should have said, 'The office is to the left, correct?'" She ruffled the child's hair. "You're so literal, aren't you?"

"What's literal?" Crystal came to her younger brother's defense.

"It means he takes words exactly as they're said." When she saw she had confused the children, she hurried to add, "He's a good listener."

Opening the door marked Office, Beth Ann led the others into a room that looked like a living room. A fireplace was set to one side with low filing cabinets in front of it. Two-thirds of the room was filled with desks, stacked boxes and cubbyholes marked with names she guessed belonged to staff. A counter was high enough for an adult to write on.

"Can I help you?" called a voice from somewhere beyond the boxes.

"The children haven't been attending school," Beth Ann replied as she watched Robert sit with the kids on a bench along the wall, "and I wanted to make sure they were still enrolled. Can you tell me whom I should talk to?"

A woman stepped around the boxes. "You can talk to me. I'm Angela Cramer, the school secretary."

Angela Cramer was a tall woman with thick glasses. Her graying hair on either side of her round face was pulled back in a stylish knot. By looking at her, Beth Ann guessed she was both kind and strict with the children at the school.

Ms. Cramer asked, "Those are the Henderson children, aren't they?"

"Yes. Douglas, Crystal and Tommy Henderson."

Ms. Cramer bent to retrieve a folder from beneath the counter. "So you must be Beth Ann Overholt."

"Yes."

"I'd heard you'd taken them in." She lowered her voice as she put the folder on the counter. "A lot of people are grateful you have. Those kids should never have been left alone. If we'd had any idea…"

She shook her head and opened the file. "Tommy isn't registered for school. Is he five?"

"He will be on Christmas Day."

"The cutoff for kindergartners is November first. If they're not five, they have to wait another year." Ms. Cramer smiled. "You could put him in the day care center at the church. Gwen O'Malley is excellent at getting little ones prepared for kindergarten. She mentioned the other day she's got openings. I'm sure Tommy would enjoy it there."

"My sister's girls go there," Robert said, surprising her because she hadn't heard him come to stand behind her. "Thanks for the suggestion."

"Glad to help." She pushed a button on the wall by the cubbyholes, then a second one.

Within a minute, an elderly woman came into the office. She was introduced as the teacher assistant who would escort the two older children to their classrooms. Again, Dougie looked obstinate and Crystal eager.

Telling them that she'd be back to pick them up at the end of the school day, Beth Ann gave each of them a quick kiss on the forehead and watched as they left. Tommy's eyes began to fill with tears until she told him that she had a special surprise for him once they were done in the office. His grin returned.

She turned back to the counter as Ms. Cramer said, "Let's get this paperwork filled out. You sign here, Robert. The mayor explained you'd be taking care of the children, too." Ms. Cramer smiled. "I've got to tell you she's pleased to hear you'll be helping Beth Ann with the children. She had lots of good things to say about you."

Beth Ann read disbelief on his face. Why would he think the mayor would bad-mouth him? Remembering how he'd exchanged words with Gladys about the covered bridge, she realized he thought the mayor would resent him for speaking his mind. She wanted to tell him that was stupid, people didn't act like that.

His expression warned he wouldn't believe her. She couldn't help wondering who had left him hurt and distrustful.

"Mayor Whittaker vouched for me?" Robert put one hand on the edge of the counter, needing something to connect him to reality. He hadn't expected the mayor to give him a character reference. Not a *gut* one, at any rate. While he'd helped Beth Ann and the *kinder* move into the apartment, he'd found ways to avoid the mayor so she couldn't remind him how weak his grip on his temper was.

"She did." The woman's glasses rose on her apple-red cheeks as she smiled. "Said you were willing to do whatever was necessary to help the town, and it seems as if you found a good cause to get behind. It's a shame what's happened to those kids."

Before Ms. Cramer could add anything else, the phone rang. She went to a desk flanked by two tall filing cabinets.

Robert held the door for Beth Ann and Tommy before shutting it behind himself. He heard familiar voices and looked between the temporary classrooms to see Dougie with the teacher's aide, frowning. Did the boy have a real reason for not wanting to be in school, or was he annoyed the adults in his life insisted he attend?

Beth Ann would have to ferret it out of the boy. Dougie didn't speak to Robert unless necessary. Maybe it was for the best the *kinder* weren't getting attached to him. He'd spent more time with them in the past few days than he could afford. Putting off searching for a job much longer would be stupid when his *daed*'s debts needed to be paid by June. He had no idea how he'd earn enough to reimburse the man, and he didn't want to ask his sisters to bail him out.

He knew he was going to disappoint Beth Ann, but he had no idea how else to pay his *daed*'s debts and begin his life anew without that shadow lurking over him.

Chapter Six

Beth Ann wasn't surprised when, as they walked away from the school trailers, Robert said he had to get to work. She asked him to tell the others she wouldn't be there that day because she had to arrange for Tommy to be enrolled at the day care center. With a curt nod, Robert strode toward Washboard Brook and the new houses north of the center of Evergreen Corners.

He acted as if he couldn't wait to get away from her and the children. Guilt tugged at her. Had she forced him into helping because she was overwhelmed with being responsible for three children? He'd come to Evergreen Corners to help rebuild, and he was assisting with finishing the apartments in David Riehl's barn. In addition, he wanted to make sure the covered bridge didn't collapse. Instead of respecting how much he had on his mind, she'd roped him into helping her with the kids.

Somehow, she needed to apologize to him for assuming he had the time and energy to help. While she'd been praying for God to show her a way to move forward with her life, his prayers were very different.

She shuddered. If she apologized, would he think that she didn't want him to help further? She must choose her words with care. She didn't want the children to feel as if they were being abandoned again.

You enjoy his company, too, chided her conscience.

Robert could be prickly, but he wasn't able to hide his generous heart. He'd come to Evergreen Corners to volunteer and make a difference.

Tommy tugged on her sleeve, yanking her from her thoughts. "Me next?"

"You are next," she said with a smile. She

swung their hands as they walked along the sidewalk bordered by icy snow.

Watching his uneven steps, she asked, "Have you ever seen a brace like mine, Tommy?"

He glanced at her leg, then shook his head. "Nope."

"So you've never worn one, too?"

"Nope." Confusion knitted his forehead.

Not wanting to upset the little boy, she changed the subject to Thanksgiving, which was the following week. She asked about what he wanted to eat and laughed when he suggested quesadillas.

"Quesadillas for Thanksgiving? That's interesting."

Bouncing from one foot to the other and swaying on his weak leg, he said, "Yummy, too." Without a pause, he asked, "What's a quesadilla?"

Again she chuckled. "Sort of like a grilled cheese sandwich but with a tortilla instead of bread. You haven't ever had one?"

He shook his head. "I heard someone talking about them."

"Well, we'll have to try making some. Not for Thanksgiving, because I don't think I'd like them with turkey."

"Okay," he said before he began chattering about everything around them as they walked to the small white church near the bridge at the village's heart. He was interested in the activity at the old mill. It was the last building on the four corners that hadn't reopened, but the mill, which housed artists and artisans, was scheduled to open its doors soon.

"I don't know," Beth Ann had to say more than once as he asked questions about the building. She didn't know what had been made there. She didn't know if there would be shops selling candy or ice cream. "I'll try to find out."

That seemed to satisfy him because the little boy began to talk about how fun it was to drop branches off the bridge and watch them zip away on the current between the ice edging both banks like the crust of a half-eaten pie.

Tommy became silent as Beth Ann led

him into the cellar of the church. His voice vanished when they were enfolded by the sounds of other children, happy children who were singing what she guessed was a nursery rhyme.

The room was decorated in a rainbow of colors splashed across the tables and the chairs, the pictures on the walls, and rubber tiles on the floor. One of the half dozen children pointed toward them, and a woman who must be Gwen O'Malley smiled at them. In her long denim skirt and simple blouse, she looked plain. She didn't wear a *kapp* and her hair, as red as Tommy's, was loose around her shoulders.

Beth Ann introduced herself and Tommy and explained why they were there.

Gwen nodded, her sympathetic eyes becoming cheerful. "Of course, we'd love to have Tommy join us."

"The paperwork—"

"Can be filled out when you come to pick him up." Gwen's smile widened. "We're having fun, and this would be a good time for Tommy to join us."

With a grateful smile, Beth Ann bent to tell Tommy he was going to stay and she was leaving.

His lower lip began to tremble. "Don't leave me, too," he moaned.

She closed her eyes as his pain battered her heart. "I'm coming back, Tommy. I promise."

"Aunt Sharon said that."

"I *am* coming back. If I don't pick you up, who will help me frost the cake for dessert tonight?"

His face brightened. "Don't forget!"

"I won't." She'd stop at the village's general store and get confectioner's sugar to make a simple buttercream frosting to spread on a layer cake that had been waiting in a box on the landing that morning. She should be able to manage not to mess it up.

"I get penders?"

"Let's see what happens after we decorate the cake." She had no idea what he meant, but maybe she'd guess by the time she picked him up. "Okay?"

"Okay."

"So you'll stay with us?" asked Gwen as she held out her hand.

Tommy grasped it. "Do you have crayons?"

"Lots and lots," she said with a laugh.

"And pretty paper?"

"Take a look around, Tommy. We've got a lot of crayons and paper."

"Dougie and Crystal made pictures at school. Mommy used to put them on the fridge. I want to make *you* pictures, Beth Ann. Will you put them on the fridge, too?"

"I'd be honored to decorate our kitchen with your pictures, Tommy."

The little boy chattered with Gwen as if they were best friends.

Beth Ann left while he was distracted. At the small general store not far from the library, she discovered they didn't sell confectioner's sugar. She didn't have time to go to the big grocery store at the edge of town. Her dismay must have shown, because the young girl behind the counter suggested she might be able to borrow some from the community center kitchen.

Thanking her for the suggestion, Beth Ann headed in that direction. She'd take the sugar to the apartment, giving herself the chance to put in a load of laundry. She'd have a head start on the chore she needed to have done if the kids were going to have something clean to wear tomorrow. They needed more clothing, but it would have to wait until the first check arrived from DCF.

She paused to stamp snow off her boots. She opened the door and was about to call a greeting, but halted when she saw a group gathered in the main room. The women—all plain except for one *Englisch* woman—looked up from their sewing machines.

"I'm sorry," she said. "I didn't mean to interrupt."

"You aren't interrupting." Abby Kauffman, who oversaw the kitchen volunteers, stood. Her right cheek was streaked with whatever she'd been baking in the kitchen for the evening meal.

"What's going on?"

"A project aimed at keeping you out of the laundry room every day. Robert told his sister and me you've been spending too much time there."

"I don't understand."

Abby flung her hand toward the tables holding stacks of clothing. "Those have been donated by folks in town. We're making sure they'll fit Dougie, Crystal and Tommy. The buttons are being sewn on and the seams secured."

Beth Ann put her fingers to her lips to hold in her gasp. There must have been enough clothing for a dozen children. "The children are growing fast. They'll outgrow these clothes before you know it."

"Don't worry," said the elderly *Englisch* woman. "We're leaving nice big hems so they can be let down. I taught that lesson in my home ec classes."

Abby chuckled. "That's right, Doris." To Beth Ann, she added, "Doris taught sewing and cooking classes at the high school. She's our expert. By the time we're finished following her instructions, each of your children will have enough clothes to last them a week or two."

"Thank you." For the first time in more than a year, Beth Ann felt as if she belonged somewhere with people who cared about her. She hadn't known how alone she'd felt in the wake of her grandmother's death and the loss of her clinic.

And she realized something else. Robert had instigated this to help her and the children. It wasn't the act of a man who wanted to wash his hands of three troublesome kids and one demanding woman.

Warmth swept over her, and tears rolled down her cheeks. As Abby gave her a hug, Beth Ann hurried to reassure her and the other women she was crying with joy. They teased her about how she'd be able to spend her time when she wasn't doing laundry.

She welcomed the jokes because they were a sign she was becoming a true part of the plain community in Evergreen Corners. The laughter also concealed her delight at learning she hadn't coerced Robert into helping. His sympathy for the hours she devoted to laundry and how he'd stepped up without any fanfare to help kept her smiling the rest of the day.

Robert paused on the street and looked in the direction of the covered bridge. Clouds were low, and with the earlier sunset, the bridge was obscured in twilight. He didn't want to think about the disappointing discussion with Glen Landis earlier.

The bridge was worth saving, though the recovery project manager had guessed the town would need to put in millions of dollars even if the state agreed to pay for the rest of the repairs. Robert wasn't going to give up. The battered bridge refused to give in. It spoke to him in a way he hadn't expected. He'd been beaten, too, but he'd weathered his *daed*'s outbursts. Since his return to Evergreen Corners, he'd spent so much time staring at the structure and wandering around on it that he could re-create every inch by memory.

Just as he could Beth Ann's face.

The realization shook him. Too often during the day, thoughts of her slipped into his mind. Sometimes, it was when he heard her voice or her laughter from another room, but images of her smile too frequently managed to sneak into his head. Every effort to halt it had been worthless.

Heading to the community center, he intended to surround himself with other people, people who could help him keep his mind off Beth Ann and the *kinder*. He'd lose himself in talk of work and the weather and anything but a woman with remarkable green eyes.

He opened the door and stepped inside, drawing in the delicious aroma of roasted chicken and fresh *kaffi*. As he started to shrug off his coat, he heard his name called from the kitchen.

His sister Rachel rushed to him. Her hair beneath her white *kapp* was as black as his, but she was short while he towered over everyone around them. However, anyone who underestimated his sister because of her size was put to rights. She was, without question, one of the smartest people he'd ever met. Her ability to look at a problem and find a solution was one he envied.

So why haven't you told her about Daed*'s debts and how you're struggling to find a way to repay them*?

He ignored that question as he smiled and greeted her. "Where are the girls? They can eat with me, if you'd like. I'm getting quite a bit of experience in helping the little *kinder* with their meals."

His nieces were younger than the Henderson kids, but the skills he'd learned helping Tommy would serve as well with little Loribeth and Eva.

"*Danki*, but the girls have already eaten." She crooked a finger and turned. "*Komm* with me. I've got a job for you."

His heart kicked up its speed, but he reminded himself she had no idea he needed a job and how fruitless his efforts of asking around town had been. "Now?"

"*Ja.*" She hooked her arm through his. "Don't look so glum, little brother."

"What do you need me to do?" He went

into the kitchen and waved to the women working under Abby's supervision.

Rachel pointed to two large grocery bags on a table. "Take those to Beth Ann's."

"What?"

"You were here when she brought Dougie Henderson in, and you saw how much he liked chicken and biscuits. We're having it again for supper tonight, so Abby thought we should send some to Beth Ann and the *kinder.*"

"Abby thought, did she?"

Rachel flushed. "There's enough for them…and for you, if you'd like."

"Playing matchmaker, ain't so?"

"Me?" She shook her head. "You know how much I disliked it when Abby tried to play matchmaker for me and Isaac."

If his sister hadn't…? Abby ducked her head as she went to check something on the stove. Maybe his sister wasn't trying to interfere, but Abby hadn't given up her matchmaking ways.

He considered telling them they had the wrong man. He halted himself. The *kinder* had enjoyed the chicken and biscuits the night he and Beth Ann had discovered them in the appalling house. If he refused to take the bags to the apartment, he was thinking of his own feelings, not theirs.

"All right," he said, picking up both bags by their sturdy handles.

"Tell Beth Ann to send the dishes back when they're empty." Rachel winked at him. "Or you can bring them back yourself."

"Matchmaking doesn't look *gut* on you, big sister."

She slapped his arm. "Go on. The food is getting cold."

Robert walked into the main room. Every eye focused on him as he opened the door. Was everyone in the plain community involved in Abby's matchmaking? Telling himself not to be ridiculous, he left.

The clouds lurking in a low ridge across the sky had descended to envelop the top of the mountains in a gray wool embrace. Snowflakes flew on gusts of wind cold enough for the North Pole.

Delicious scents from the bags made his stomach rumble, and he quickened his steps up the sloped street. He glanced at the windows glowing onto the mayor's front porch. No sign of her, which was just as well. The best thing he could do was deliver supper and leave.

When Robert knocked on the door, he heard eager squeals of "I'll get it."

Both Tommy and Crystal stood there as the door swung open.

"It's Robert!" Tommy shouted.

"Come in!" Crystal reached out to grab his hand, but halted when she saw the bags. "He's brought presents!"

Dougie asked from the couch, "Presents?"

Robert stepped inside as Beth Ann emerged from the bunkroom. Her arms were filled with clothing. Clothing for the *kinder*, he realized when she set it on a chair.

"Some of the ladies have been remaking clothes for the children," Beth Ann said in lieu of a greeting. "Apparently I've been complaining about doing laundry too much."

"You haven't," he replied.

"You have!" chorused three *kinder*, and the younger two began to giggle.

Tommy asked, "Any penders?"

"Penders?" She looked at the older *kinder*. "Do you know what he means?"

"Penders! Like his!" He pointed to Robert's chest before looking at Beth Ann. "He's wearing penders."

"*Sus*penders." Robert laughed.

"Want some!" Tommy pleaded. "Can I have some, please?"

She put her arm around his shoulders and gave them a squeeze. "Let's see what we can find next time at the store. What do you have there, Robert?"

"Supper." He held up the bags. "Chicken and biscuits, to be exact. Abby remembered how much you like them, so she sent servings for you. Anyone interested?"

"Yes!" shouted the *kinder*.

"They're getting tired of my lack of cooking skills," Beth Ann said with a rueful smile.

"I'm sure you—"

Dougie interrupted, "Don't say that until you've had her scorched cookies."

"I had delicious ones when you moved in."

"Gladys made those," she admitted, a pretty blush climbing her cheeks. "I've never learned to cook or bake, though I try. So this delivery from the community center kitchen is extra welcome, isn't it, kids?"

Without being asked, the kids rushed to set the table.

"There's your answer," Beth Ann said with a laugh. "You'll be staying, too, won't you, Robert? Or did you have other plans tonight?"

He appreciated her giving him a way to leave without any explanation, but he was astonished he was also annoyed she thought he needed it. He was further irritated she was right. He'd spent the walk up to the apartment planning to leave as soon as he delivered the meal.

"I'll get you a chair, Robert!" announced Crystal before he could answer.

Beth Ann started to speak, but he shook his head to let her know he was okay with the girl bringing another chair to the table.

Minutes later, they were seated around the table, their heads bowed while Beth Ann said grace. He added his own silent prayer before he lifted his head and reached for his knife and fork.

The younger *kinder* wanted to share every detail of their day, but Dougie stared at his plate and scowled. That didn't stop the older boy from shoveling food into his mouth so fast Robert had to wonder if he tasted it.

When Beth Ann stood to get the dessert included with their dinner, Robert offered to help her bring it in. He saw her amazement, and again was impressed with how much she understood about Amish ways. Men didn't help in the kitchen, but most Amish men hadn't encountered a situation like this one.

He was pleased to discover Abby had put a blueberry pie and an apple one into the bags. "Which should we have?" he asked.

"Whichever you prefer. A few days ago, I would have said the apple one, because I'm not sure I could get blueberry stains out of Tommy's clothes. Now he's got lots to wear."

He laughed along with her. Being with Beth Ann was easy tonight. In the wake of a difficult day, he appreciated her sense of humor that pushed aside worry. He guessed it was a technique she'd refined as a midwife when nervous parents awaited the arrival of their *bopplin*.

Offering to slice cheese to go along with the warm pie, he did so until a white-hot pain sliced across the index finger on his left hand. "Ouch!"

"What did you do?" she asked as she turned from where she was setting a piece of pie on a plate.

He examined his bleeding finger. "Cut it on the knife."

She held out her hand, but said nothing.

He didn't put his bloody finger on her palm. Instead, he held it up in front of her eyes. Taking his hand, she turned it one way, then the other.

"It doesn't look as if it'll need stitches, but we need to get it tended to," she said with gentle authority.

"I'm a big boy. I don't need my *mamm* bandaging my boo-boos."

She smiled. "Big boys know how important it is to get an antiseptic on a cut." She turned on the tap. "Hold it under the water while I get the first aid kit."

The icy water sent pain erupting from his finger, but he held it under the faucet, knowing she was right. He needed to get the wound clean.

She came back with a small white box. With a few deft moves, she cleaned his finger and spread ointment on the cut. She put a pad against his finger and bound it in place with gauze.

"Leave this on until tomorrow morning," she said. "You'll have to be careful when you peel the bandaging off because it probably will stick to you. If there's a problem, soak it in warm, soapy water until the bandaging loosens."

"Soapy water? What kind of soap?"

She smiled. "Dish detergent works fine, but make sure the water is clean and change it before you do the dishes."

"I would have figured that out on my own."

"You'd be surprised how many don't."

He looked from her to his finger. *"Danki."*

Putting what she'd used into the first aid box, she said, "You're welcome. Try to use the knife as it's intended, okay?"

"Ja, especially when I'm not with a midwife."

"Former midwife."

He frowned, unable to mistake the sudden emptiness in her voice. "You've given up the work?"

"I'm not licensed in Vermont." She changed the subject before he could probe further. "The kids won't be patient much longer waiting on their slices of pie." She picked up three plates and motioned for him to grab the other two.

He followed her into the main room where he served himself and Crystal. The *kinder* were as thrilled with the blueberry pie as he was, and everyone was shocked when Tommy finished every bite without dropping any on himself...until he spilled his milk in his excitement.

By the time Beth Ann had cleaned up the little boy, it was late enough to get the *kinder* ready for bed. Dougie was allowed to stay up an hour later, but he had homework to fill his time.

Robert cleaned the table, rinsed off the dishes and repacked what he'd brought in one bag. There weren't any leftovers, except for the untouched apple pie, despite Abby sending enough for a half dozen men who were starving after a long day of physical labor.

Beth Ann came into the kitchen with two chairs. She set them in the middle of the room. "Would you like another cup of coffee?"

"Too late if I want to get any sleep to-night."

"I've got decaf."

He was reluctant to let the evening end. He stared out the window, where the gentle snowstorm had become a wind-whipped swirl of ice and flakes. Thinking about the distance he had to walk to get home, he knew it would be better to have something warm inside him. "Sounds *gut*."

When she set a steaming cup and a piece of the pie on the counter beside him, he reached to close the door.

She halted him and shifted the door to where it'd been. "If you close it, I can't see any eavesdroppers."

Swallowing his chuckle, he reached for the cup and sat on the chair beside the counter. He sighed before he could halt himself.

"How was your day?" she asked.

"Okay."

"Just okay? Did something go wrong today at the project house?"

"Not at the house. I spoke with Glen about the bridge."

"Glen's a nice guy."

He took a sip of his *kaffi*. "I agree, but he reminded me his job is rebuilding homes."

"What about the bridge? It's an important structure, too, isn't it?"

"While folks are inconvenienced by having to drive out of their way, they can get in and out without the bridge. They've *got* homes. He's saving resources for those who don't. He spoke about having to get a structural engineer and experienced stonemasons and carpenters to rebuild the bridge."

"Abby's brother, Isaac, is a mason. Can't he—?"

"I've been told Isaac doesn't feel he's got the skills for what the bridge requires. He's an expert with pouring foundations for houses, not a bridge."

"Why is this so important to you?"

He almost answered her question with a trite response. He halted himself. She'd listened, even before the *kinder* brought them more deeply into each other's lives. She deserved an honest answer.

"I need the work," he said.

"More than you're already doing?"

"I need a paying job if I hope to stay in Evergreen Corners."

"Are you looking to buy a farm?"

He shook his head and laughed. "I know every Amish man is supposed to want to be a farmer, but I've had enough of that life. Old Terry—"

"Who?"

"He was our neighbor when I was about Dougie's age." He looked past her as he spoke the boy's name, but if Dougie had heard him, the boy gave no sign. "He was a woodworker, and he taught me to appreciate wood and the beautiful and useful things made from it."

She got up and refilled their cups. "So you're looking for a temporary job until you get your shop open?"

"*Ja.*" He wouldn't reveal the truth about his *daed*'s debts. His sisters would have helped. For him. Not for *Daed*. People would be curious about why they were such unloving *kinder*. Tales of his *daed*'s uncontrolled temper would emerge, and eyes would begin to watch Robert for signs he was like Manassas Yoder.

It had happened before. In Ohio when rumors of the abuse rumbled through the plain community. He didn't want to have to face scrutiny again.

Beth Ann sat. "Have you talked to Isaac himself about the bridge?"

"No."

"Instead of asking everyone else, talk to *him*. If he agrees to help, you'll be in a stronger position. If he doesn't…" She leaned forward. "I'll be praying he says yes. I mean, he says *ja*."

He guessed she was teasing him to pull him out of his bad mood, and he had to admit she was doing a great job. She was sensible, persuasive and lovely as the kitchen light lit auburn flickers through her hair. An idea popped into his head, and he gave it voice before he could convince himself not to.

"Isaac is up north. Rachel said he'll be home by Thanksgiving. *Komm* to Thanksgiving with us. She's been wanting to meet you and the *kinder*. It's the least I can do to say *danki* for bandaging my finger."

"True. It's the least *you* can do when your sister is making the meal."

He chuckled. Trading words with Beth Ann was fun. When she agreed to bring the Henderson kids, he felt something open up deep inside him, something he hadn't known existed. Happiness. Simple, thrilling happiness.

However, he warned himself he couldn't let himself enjoy her company too much. Savoring it could lead to the courtship that whispers suggested they already were sharing. He must not offer her more than friendship when he couldn't be certain when the beast of his temper would awaken.

Because his *mamm*, when she warned about how an uncontrollable temper infected all Yoder men, might not have been wrong.

Chapter Seven

Tommy didn't expect an answer from Beth Ann while he rattled off every activity he'd done since she'd taken him to day care on the morning before Thanksgiving. He was most excited about making a "turkey" by tracing his hand and coloring it.

Beth Ann smiled. The drawing meant as much to Tommy as his stuffed bear. He'd made her promise she'd put it on the fridge, and she would as soon as they reached the apartment.

Listening to him was like music after hearing the pounding of nail guns putting on shingles all afternoon. The project house was scheduled to be done in two weeks, and the volunteers were thrilled to be ready to hand the next-to-last house to its new owners. Each person became more energetic and resourceful as the finish line drew closer. Work that had seemed tedious days before was infused with excitement.

As they walked along a snowy path on the village green, Beth Ann kept an eye on the ground. Tommy's uneven steps made ice even more treacherous. She wished she could get him to see Dr. Kingsley, but Pastor Hershey had advised her to wait until the social worker assigned to the kids contacted her. She'd made sure the cell phone she'd used with patients was charged, and she carried it with her wherever she went. So far, there hadn't been a call from the social worker, Deana Etheridge, and tomorrow was a holiday.

If Tommy had to wear a brace, would he be taunted as she'd been? Would he have someone he believed might be interested in him turn away, disgusted because the plastic kept his foot from slapping the ground?

Don't think about that! she told herself

as she had every time her mind wandered
to Webster Gerig and Ted Contreras. The
men who had flirted with her after church
while she was sitting and they didn't notice her brace.

*Robert doesn't seem bothered by your
brace.*

Why couldn't her brain be quiet instead
of yakking like Tommy?

Beth Ann turned her attention to the little
boy so she could avoid confronting her own
thoughts. He was excited about showing off
his picture to his brother and sister. As they
walked along, she waved to familiar people and made sure the little boy avoided the
deepest snowbanks. He'd want to play with
his siblings after they got out of school, and
she didn't want his boots filled with snow
that would melt and refreeze when he went
outside again.

By the time she got Tommy home, had
hung up his picture on the refrigerator with
a magnet left behind by a previous ten-
ant and had him seated at the table with
fruit juice and one of Gladys's delicious

chocolate chip cookies, Crystal and Dougie arrived home. Beth Ann poured juice for them and brought the chipped rabbit cookie jar in from the kitchen. Setting the treats in the middle of the table, she waited until they'd pulled off their backpacks and hung them with their coats in the closet by the door.

"How was your day at school?" she asked as they took their seats and helped themselves to cookies and juice.

Dougie shrugged, and Crystal didn't meet her eyes.

Beth Ann sighed. She recognized those silent responses. The kids had wanted to avoid answering her questions. Pushing them would make them more stubborn and taciturn. She was curious why they didn't talk about school, but she'd save her questions until later. They remained distrustful of adults, and she couldn't blame them. They'd been abandoned by the people who should have been most concerned about them.

Her phone rang, and she pulled it from her apron pocket.

"You've got a cell phone?" asked Dougie. "I thought Amish people didn't have those."

As she put the phone to her ear, she didn't bother to remind him—again—she wasn't Amish. She held up one finger to let Dougie know she'd answer his question after she finished the call. Her hope it was Deana Etheridge vanished when a robotic voice congratulated her on being selected for a discount on a new roof.

She chuckled. The telemarketer had no idea how her ears rang from the nail gun's thumps all day.

Seeing Dougie with his arms folded and a scowl, she said, "Dougie, help me get the laundry. While we're doing that, I'll explain why I have a cell phone."

"I shoulda known you'd find a way to turn a question into chores. Will I have to help you fold it, too?"

Trying not to smile at his tone that suggested the job was a waking nightmare, she asked, "Crystal, can I count on you to fold the clothes with me?"

The girl brightened. "Can I?"

Dougie grumbled something under his breath about her being a loser.

Beth Ann decided to ignore him. When he was in such a foul mood, chastising him was futile. He became more annoyed...and more annoying.

Instead, she handed him his coat while she told Crystal to make sure neither she nor Tommy touched anything in the kitchen while she and their older brother went downstairs to the laundry room. She gave Dougie time to pull his coat on and steered him outside.

"What's this?" she asked when she saw two bags on the landing. Both were imprinted with the name of Spezio's Market, which was located outside Evergreen Corners.

"Looks like groceries." Dougie peered into one bag. "Yep, there are two cans of chili in this one along with other stuff." He gave a cheer. "Refried beans! We can have tacos tonight!" He paused and asked, "Do you know how to make tacos without burning them?"

Instead of answering, she asked, "Is there a note or a receipt?"

He pawed through the bags. "Nope. Nothing."

Beth Ann scanned the narrow sections of sidewalk and green she could see. This wasn't the first time groceries had appeared at the top of the stairs. When she'd queried those she thought might be arranging for the delivery—Pastor Hershey, the mayor, Abby, Robert—each of them had been as surprised as she was by the unknown benefactor's generosity.

Who was sending groceries to the apartment?

"Thank you," she said so her words would reach the street.

"You are so weird." Douglas opened the door and put the bags inside.

"You're just figuring that out?" She laughed as she went down the stairs.

"So why do you have a phone?"

"Because families having babies needed to be able to get in touch with me."

"You're not doing that here."

"No, but I need to be on call for other things." She saw the questions in his eyes, but ducked into the garage before he could ask. Talking to the children about DCF and the social worker bothered her and was sure to upset them.

The laundry room was warmer than the garage. As she opened the door to the dryer stacked on the washing machine, Beth Ann sent up another prayer of gratitude the mayor had put a laundry in the garage for her tenants' use.

Dougie wasn't interested in answering her questions. She gave up and, after cleaning the lint trap, handed him one of the two small baskets to carry while she switched another load of clothing from the washer to the dryer. It was the final one for the day.

She took the other basket and followed the boy upstairs, picking up the stray sock or T-shirt that fell from his basket. She was glad none dropped through the open steps onto the snow below, because she didn't want to remain outside in the cold any longer than necessary.

Dougie left the basket in the middle of the floor and strode into the children's bedroom to play with Tommy.

Dumping her own load on the bed in her room, Beth Ann picked up two of Tommy's socks and rolled them together. Crystal came in and tried to do the same. When the girl found the task frustrating, Beth Ann asked her to match up the socks and set them on the bed, so they could be rolled up later.

"Hey, Crystal!" called Tommy from the other room. "Come and see!"

The girl paused, torn.

"Go ahead," Beth Ann said with a smile. "I can finish the rest."

Tossing the socks onto the clothing, Crystal ran to join her brothers.

Beth Ann hummed to herself as she finished folding and sorting the clothing from her basket. She got the other basket and continued with the task, checking each garment for holes and wear. Again she was thankful for what had been donated to the family, because the children were hard on their clothing.

"As they should be when they're being children," she said to herself, reaching for a pair of Crystal's jeans.

Something fluttered to the bed. The kids never remembered to empty their pockets. She checked, but occasionally missed something. She hadn't seen any bits of paper mixed in with the lint, and this item appeared to be intact.

It was money! She uncrumpled the single bill. A twenty! How had that gotten into the laundry? Had she stuffed it in a pocket while at the store? No, being careful with money was something her grandmother had taught her.

If it wasn't hers, how had it gotten into the dryer?

She went into the other bedroom. The children were building a tower already taller than Tommy. She explained what she'd found and asked if they knew where the bill had come from.

They denied any knowledge of it. She

wanted to believe them, because she had no idea how kids who'd lived in squalor and hadn't had enough to eat would have twenty dollars.

"Maybe it belongs to Gladys," Beth Ann said when she realized nobody was going to admit they knew about the money. "I'll stop by tomorrow and give it to her."

"You're giving her twenty dollars?" Dougie grimaced. "She'll keep it."

"I can't keep what's not mine."

"Finders keepers, right?"

"What if it were you?"

"I don't have twenty dollars."

"What if you did, and you lost it? Wouldn't you want the person who found it to return the money instead of spending it?"

The boy didn't fire back a quick, sass-filled answer. Instead, he said, "Lady Bee, if I ever get my hands on twenty dollars, I'd be stupid to lose it."

"I'm sure you would be." She put the bill in her pocket.

"What will you do with it if it's not the mayor's?" Crystal asked.

"I think it'd make a nice donation at church on Sunday, don't you?"

When the three children exchanged a quick glance, she guessed they didn't agree with her. She waited for one of them to share how the money had gotten into the laundry. None of them did.

Tomorrow was Thanksgiving. During the visit to Robert's sister's house, she'd talk to him about what had happened. Maybe he would have a suggestion of the best way to get to the truth.

Beth Ann was glad to see the lights from the old farmhouse as she drove up the lane, the excited children in the back seat. The sun had set an hour ago, and the night was bitterly cold. As she stepped out of her car, she pulled her red-and-blue-striped scarf closer to her face. She checked each child to make sure they still were bundled up, helped Tommy out of his borrowed car seat and herded them toward the house.

The steps creaked a warning as they climbed. A bright orange road cone marked a spot where the porch floor had given way, and she watched the boards uneasily. The children must have noticed, too, because they tiptoed toward the door.

It opened, and a woman who was a head shorter than Beth Ann called out, "It's not as bad as it looks. Isaac found that cone in the barn and left it on the porch so he'll remember to take it to the town barn." She laughed. "Maybe he will remember one of these days."

"I'm glad to hear that." She smiled at the woman whose hair was as black as a star-studded sky.

"*Komm* in. I'm Rachel Yoder, and you must be Elizabeth Overholt." She took a step back to let Beth Ann enter. Her blue eyes were warm with welcome.

"Beth Ann, please."

She grinned at the Henderson children. "Dougie, Crystal and Tommy. Is that right?"

"Yep!" shouted the irrepressible Tommy. "Do you have cows?"

"Not in the house," Rachel replied while she put her hands on the shoulders of two little girls peeking around her dark green skirt. "I do have my daughters. This is Loribeth, and the little one is Eva."

"Me Eva!" She grabbed Tommy's hand. "*Komm* see my kitty."

"*Our* kitty," corrected her older sister with the weary tone of someone who'd had to repeat herself too often.

"Take our guests," Rachel said, "and play with Sweetie Pie while I get supper on the table. Beth Ann and I are going to talk."

Eva pouted for a moment, then brightened. "Play with my—our kitty."

As the two girls scampered away with the younger Henderson children, Beth Ann looked at Dougie. "You don't want to go and play, too?"

"Not with little kids."

Rachel said, "Isaac and Robert are out in the big barn. Why don't you join them?"

"Go ahead," Beth Ann seconded when she saw how excited he was to be counted among the men. "Don't touch anything without asking first."

Dougie rolled his eyes, then scurried out before she could change her mind.

"Thanks," Beth Ann said. She unbuttoned her coat and slipped it off, savoring the scents of stuffing and roasting turkey.

"Robert is supposed to be helping you, so I thought I'd let him have the opportunity to do so." Rachel gave a conspiratorial laugh, and Beth Ann knew Robert's sister enjoyed picking on her brother.

Beth Ann noticed, other than the kitchen, the house wasn't in much better shape inside than outside, but it was clean. Though the kitchen floor was gouged and had lost any finish it might once have had, the maple cupboards shone with attention. The refrigerator gleamed beneath the collection of childish drawings hanging on the door. A huge woodstove claimed one side of the room, giving off a welcoming heat. A pair of pots steamed on a gas range that must be older than she was. In the middle of the room, a long table was set for ten, but could have comfortably held half again that number.

"What can I do to help?" she asked as she hung up her coat on the row of pegs by the door. She knew any woman invited to join an Amish family for a meal was expected to pitch in.

"Can you cut the bread and put it and butter on the table?"

"Gladly." Had Robert warned her that Beth Ann had few skills in the kitchen?

Picking up the knife, she sliced two loaves of warm bread. As she had often in the past, she asked herself why she could wield a knife with ease, but couldn't boil an egg without burning the pot. Though her grandmother had taught her the skills to become a midwife, Grandmother Overholt's attempts to teach her to cook had ended in failure.

She glanced into the living room as she walked to the table. The children were sitting on the floor, surrounded by books. Crystal was reading aloud to her brother and Rachel's daughters. They were the picture of perfect domestic harmony, and Beth Ann knew, whatever she decided about her future, she wanted having a family to be part of it. Losing her grandmother had left a far bigger void in her life than having her job disrupted.

She didn't begrudge Rachel her beautiful family, but oh, how she longed to have one of her own! She was happy, despite the challenges of taking care of the Henderson children. The youngsters were becoming her family to replace the one she'd lost. No, *replace* wasn't the right word, but she longed to belong with someone else again.

God, is that what You want for me? She looked at the brace on her leg, wondering again whether there was a man out there who wouldn't see it as a reason for her to make an unsuitable wife and mother.

The door opened again, and Robert walked in with Dougie and a man Beth Ann knew was Isaac Kauffman. Cold air flowed in with them, and Rachel chided them to close the door. The children rushed into the kitchen, followed by a tiny calico kitten with the biggest front paws Beth Ann had ever seen on a cat.

She was more amazed to discover her gaze wanted to linger on Robert. With his face slapped red by the cold, its strong lines were emphasized. Her fingers tingled at the thought of tracing from one craggy plane to the next.

What was she thinking? She wasn't a teenager who couldn't control her hormones. She was a grown woman, too grown for most men to take a second glance at. Robert Yoder was a compelling man, and from glances she'd seen at the community center, he could have had his pick of the single plain women in Evergreen Corners. Letting herself imagine otherwise was foolish, so why couldn't she stop thinking of a future the two of them could share?

Robert sat at the kitchen table between his niece Eva and Dougie while they bowed their heads for grace. Dougie had been thrilled to discover Clipper in the barn, and he'd asked when Robert would teach him to drive. When Robert said he wasn't sure, the boy kept pestering him while Robert tried to keep his temper from rising at the incessant interruptions.

Isaac had stepped in with his usual quiet dignity. "Dougie, I know it's not easy to wait, but that's what God often asks of us. In Psalm 37, it says: 'Rest in the Lord, and wait patiently for Him: fret not thyself because of him who prospereth in his way, because of the man who bringeth wicked devices to pass. Cease from anger, and forsake wrath: fret not thyself in any wise to do evil.'"

Had Isaac looked at Robert while speaking the second verse about anger and wrath? Or was it his own shame that made the words resonate?

"Why is Beth Ann's *kapp* not like my *mamm*'s?" asked Eva as she tugged on his sleeve, banishing the unpleasant memory.

"Your mother is Amish," Beth Ann said with a smile before he could. "I'm Mennonite." Seeing the child didn't understand, she pointed at Rachel's pleated *kapp*.

"That's what your family wears, and this is what my family wears."

"Like your shoehorn?" The little girl peered under the table.

For a moment, Beth Ann was confused. "Oh, my brace!"

"Eva, what have I told you about talking about what people look like?" asked Rachel, a flush climbing her cheeks.

Beth Ann chuckled. "Everyone is curious about my brace, but only children are forthright enough to come out and ask."

Robert averted his eyes. He'd glanced often at her brace, but never had found the words to ask her about it. When she hadn't offered any explanation, he'd assumed she didn't want to discuss it.

He'd been wrong, because she spoke to his niece as easily as if they'd been discussing the cat. "I hurt my leg when I was in an accident when I was four years old."

"Does it hurt?"

Rachel scolded again. "Eva, enough."

"It's okay," Beth Ann reassured her before saying to the little girl, "No, my leg doesn't hurt, but the brace makes me itch sometimes when it's hot."

The answer tickled the little girl, who giggled.

Her mother turned to Isaac and Robert. "The living room is ready to be painted whenever you two have time."

"Beth Ann is an experienced painter," Robert said, his smile returning. "Or so she's told me."

"You're not going to pass the task off to her when she's already got her hands full." Rachel wagged a finger at him, then looked at Beth Ann. "The girls and I are staying here while we make the house livable. Our trailer was damaged in the tornado during the last hurricane."

"Can we move in, too?" asked Dougie, stabbing another big slice of turkey off the platter in front of him. "This food is great! Beth Ann is nice, but her cooking..." He gulped and lowered his head.

The room grew still until Beth Ann laughed. She patted Dougie's arm. "I think

I'll be asking Rachel for her recipes and her advice on how to prepare them."

"Quesadillas?" asked Tommy.

That drew chuckles from the adults and more giggles from the youngsters.

The uncomfortable moment passed, but Robert found himself glancing at Beth Ann when the conversation shifted to the old mill's reopening next week. Her lips were tilted in a smile, but a hint of shadow clung to her eyes. Though he wanted to ask what was bothering her, he didn't. He didn't want to force her into being the center of attention again.

"Are you planning to go to the mill's open house next week, Beth Ann?" Isaac asked.

"Everyone's been talking about it, and I'm curious to see it."

"Doris Blomgren will be giving classes on advanced sewing techniques." Rachel smiled. "I've got to figure out how to make seams little girls won't burst the first time they go out to play."

"Who's Doris?" Robert asked.

"She helped," his sister replied, "with the

project to remake the donated clothing for our young friends."

"And those seams are still intact." Beth Ann laughed. "In spite of being worn by three very active kids."

Again laughter swirled around the table, the sound of friends and family enjoying their time together.

When the meal was finished, the *kinder*, including Dougie this time, went into the living room to play with the kitten and color in the books Rachel pulled out of a basket. The Henderson kids helped his nieces find the picture they wanted and offered them the first choice of crayons.

"Robert, why don't you and Beth Ann sit and chat while Isaac helps me put away the leftovers?" asked Rachel.

"I can help," Beth Ann offered. "I may not be a great cook, but I'm a skilled dishwasher."

"Me, too," Robert said.

Rachel waved her hands at them. "Go, go! You're my guests, and I'm not asking my guests to do the dishes."

Robert was about to argue when he noticed a furtive glance between his sister and Isaac. It told him the two of them wanted time alone.

Beth Ann must have seen it, too, because she motioned for him to follow her toward the door. "We'll bring in some wood, so you won't have to go out later, Rachel."

"*Danki,*" his sister said, but she was already turning toward the man she planned to marry.

Grabbing his coat and Beth Ann's, he waited until she'd buttoned hers and pulled on her gloves and hat. He opened the door and led the way out into the blustery twilight. Edging around the weakest boards on the porch, he motioned for her to follow him through the frigid evening toward the woodpile on the far side of the house.

He started to apologize for his niece's nosy queries, but Beth Ann waved his words aside.

"I don't mind answering a child's questions," she said. "Eva was curious, and she asked. That's what we want children to do."

"Not adults?"

Her lips tightened, and his heart beat three times before she answered, "I don't mind answering an adult's questions, either, if the questions are asked in the same way Eva's were."

"You mean wanting to learn more without judgment?"

She bent to pick up a chunk of wood and put it on his outstretched arms. "Questions that judge and try to belittle I despise." Lifting another piece, she faced him as she held it to her like a *boppli*. "Tommy's gait could be helped by a brace, but I can't keep from wondering if it'll be the source of prejudice against him as he grows up."

"Like it was for you?"

"At times. What do you think?"

"You've been around us Amish enough to know we don't look at disabilities the way the rest of the world does."

She nodded, her eyes glistening like the twinkling stars above them. "I've seen babies born with horrible birth defects, but they were welcomed into their family for as long as they lived. Nobody complained about the care or cost of that care. They simply loved those children."

"We call them special."

"You mean the child is a special, wondrous gift from God."

"We each are a special, *wunderbaar* gift from God." He set the wood she'd handed him on the edge of the porch and put his hands on her arms.

Touching her was a mistake, he knew. When he looked down into her warm eyes, they brightened in an unspoken invitation. What would happen if he drew her to him and sampled her lips?

Nothing, his mind warned him.

Nothing would happen because nothing could happen. What could he offer her other than a man whose only inheritance from his *daed* had been a vile temper?

He released her. Picking up the wood, he added a few chunks before he walked up the stairs and into the house. He sensed her gaze following every step.

A gaze filled with bafflement and hurt. If

he'd given in to his yearning to kiss her and make her more of a part of his life, her gaze might change to regret. He had enough regrets in his life already. He didn't need to be burdened with the fact that he'd caused more for her.

Chapter Eight

The day had been a mess from the moment Robert woke to discover the furnace in David Riehl's barn had stopped working. His teeth chattered, and the water in a glass he kept by his bed had a coat of ice. He'd tried to get it started again. It didn't work. He'd woken David to alert him so the pipes didn't freeze.

Helping fix the furnace had made him too late to stop for breakfast, so he'd gone directly to the project house. The volunteers were in an uproar because someone had broken in during the Thanksgiving break. Tools left there as well as small decorative items had vanished. There had been other thefts from the project houses, but this one had also resulted in two windows being broken and their screens warped. It would take at least a couple of days to get those replaced.

Mutters about who might be responsible and what should be done to keep it from happening again had left a cloud over the cheerful workplace. Inattention led to a series of accidents from paint being dumped onto the new floors to sections of molding being miscut, so the wood was wasted. People who'd worked together for weeks with the skill and precision of a team of horses plowing a field bumped into one another again and again.

What seemed worst, however, was that Beth Ann didn't come to work that day. Nobody seemed to know why. Was one of the *kinder* ill? Was Beth Ann? He hadn't seen or spoken to her since Thanksgiving, and their last words had been terse and tense. He hadn't been avoiding her.

Well, not exactly.

It'd been easy to use the excuse of being

exhausted not to stop by the apartment. Or needing to work to finish walls and floors in exchange for staying in David's barn. More than once, he'd considered confiding in her that he was making furniture for David's place as well, using the skills Old Terry had taught him. Working with wood was what he longed to do, whether repairing the covered bridge or creating a table using scraps he found around the farm.

Robert tried not to think of how much he missed talking with Beth Ann and teasing the *kinder*. He needed to focus on his work. He held his tongue the first half dozen times someone elbowed him or almost hit him with a length of wood, but when an empty plastic bucket dropped on his head, his temper burst forth.

"Be careful!" he snapped as he stood, rubbing his skull.

The woman on the ladder was, he realized when his eyes focused, Vera. "You shouldn't have been under my feet."

"Don't blame me because *you're* careless!" he shouted before he could halt himself.

Tears filled her eyes. "I'm sorry."

His hateful temper diminished, but it'd already done damage. Frowns were aimed in his direction. Wishing he could take back the serrated words, he hurried to accept Vera's apology and offer one of his own.

She accepted it, but said nothing more.

He hung his aching head and returned to his work. Though a few people asked him if he was okay, most gave him a wide berth.

The Yoder temper had betrayed him yet again. *Lord, help me overcome it.* He'd made that prayer many times, and he was waiting for God to step in and help him. Until He did, Robert must be extra cautious. If not, he might turn out like his *daed* and hurt someone with more than words.

Though Beth Ann and the children arrived a half hour before the ribbon cutting was to take place at the old mill, a crowd had already gathered outside its main entry. She wondered if the locals were more interested in seeing the shops or celebrating that the final victim in Evergreen Corners had been rebuilt and was about to reopen.

The next-to-last victim.

She turned to look toward the battered covered bridge a short distance up the brook. In the dying light of the day, its silhouette resembled a skeleton with its ribs and broken bones displayed. She saw a motion near it and recognized Robert's strong-shouldered stance.

Was he the only one who couldn't pretend not to notice the sad sight?

Yes, he was. Everyone around her chattered about what might be found inside the repaired mill building. They acted as if everything was the way it had been, maybe a bit better.

Sorrow threatened to smother her. Though Robert had insisted his interest in repairing the bridge had to do with having a job with a paycheck, she knew his yearning to have it fixed went beyond dollars and cents. His face softened when he spoke of working with wood. He could see what the covered bridge once was, and he longed to return it to its former beauty.

When they first met by the bridge, she hadn't imagined the stern man could harbor such a gentle and artistic heart. There must be some reason he hid it, and she couldn't help being curious why.

Her musings were interrupted as Tommy asked her when the doors would open and Crystal pointed to a glass star in one of the upper windows and Dougie stamped his feet as he grumbled about waiting outside in the cold.

As Gladys stepped forward to cut the white-and-gold ribbon draped across the doors, Robert came through the crowd to stand beside them. The younger kids greeted him, and Beth Ann had to hush them so the mayor's words could be heard.

Gladys realized everyone was cold, so she hastily congratulated those who'd helped rebuild the mill and urged every- one to enjoy the open house. Taking a pair of oversize scissors from her husband, she clipped the ribbon.

The villagers surged forward, taking Beth Ann, Robert and the children with them. She smiled when she stepped into the welcoming warmth inside the old building. Thick pine boards were polished, but showed wear from hard use through the years. The expanse, which once had been open from one end to the other, was broken up by walls that didn't reach to the ceiling. Lights hung from gantries to brighten the individual shops and the broad hallway.

Standing to one side to let the press of people pass, Beth Ann said, "The mayor's remarks were quick. I'm sure that will earn her extra votes if people remember the cold this evening."

Robert's face lit with a smile, and she was thankful she could ease the grief plaguing him each time he went to the bridge. "Where to first?"

The wrong question, because each child had a different idea. They decided to visit the shops to their right first and the ones on their left on the way back.

"Soon all three stories will be open,"

Dougie announced. "They're going to have space to teach art on the second floor."

"And on the third?" Beth Ann asked.

"A multi-porpoise room," Crystal announced. "Aren't porpoises dolphins?"

"Multi-*purpose*." She grinned at the girl. "It means the room can be used for lots of different things."

"No fishies?" asked Tommy.

Not wanting to get into the fact that dolphins weren't fish, Beth Ann gave him another smile. "Not tonight."

She'd thought he'd ask another question, but his attention was caught by a shop selling fudge. She was surprised anyone in the hall could see anything. Clumps of people who'd stopped to talk clogged the corridor. She found herself saying, "Excuse me" as she bumped into people and shopping bags.

Looking at Robert, who'd picked up Tommy before he got stepped on, she said, "Maybe we should come back another time."

"I think that's a *gut* idea."

Suddenly Crystal ran toward a shop with

a bright sign outside announcing Your Perfect Princess Fashions.

"I'll get her." Beth Ann didn't try calling after the girl because she doubted Crystal would hear through the cacophony of excited voices.

The shop was a girl's fantasy come to life. Every dress looked as if it had been made from spun dreams in pale pinks, blues and yellows. Crinolines that hadn't been in style since long before Beth Ann was born plumped the skirts until they stood straight out from the contrasting ribbons around the waists.

"So pretty," breathed Crystal without turning. "Have you ever seen anything like them, Lady Bee?"

She was astounded Crystal knew she'd give chase. Were the kids beginning to feel she was a part of their lives?

Thank you, God, for this chance to be with them now. I know it is temporary, and I know the pain will be monstrous when I have to tell them goodbye. Please help me be as grateful through the pain as I am at this moment.

She put her arm around Crystal's shoulders. "They are fancy, aren't they?"

The girl reached out to run her finger along the smocking on one of the dresses. Her happy smile vanished when a woman yanked the dress away from the rack, scowling at Crystal.

"Don't touch it!" the woman ordered.

Crystal's eyes welled with tears.

"She was just looking," Beth Ann said.

The woman said something under her breath, and Beth Ann shuddered as she heard "light-fingered" and "troublemakers like their mother."

Sorrow filled her, wiping away her happiness. Old rumors, whether true or false, about the Henderson family were harder to erase from Evergreen Corners than the scars from the floods.

"Let's go, Crystal," Beth Ann said, taking the girl's hand as other shoppers stopped to stare. Sympathy blossomed in many eyes, but nobody stepped forward to defend

Crystal. Realizing most had no idea what had set the woman off, Beth Ann smiled at them while she took the child into the busy hallway.

Dougie pushed past other people to get to his upset sister. He glared into the shop until the woman who'd chastised Crystal lowered her eyes.

Beth Ann looked at Robert, who shared her surprise at the woman's reaction. Was she embarrassed at her own actions? Would she apologize to Crystal? The woman turned away to speak to a customer, now acting as if nothing out of the ordinary had happened.

Squatting in front of Crystal, Beth Ann drew a tissue out of her purse and handed it to the girl, who was sniffling as she struggled not to cry.

Crystal blew her nose. "Some people aren't nice."

"I'm sorry," Beth Ann said, smoothing the girl's wispy bangs.

Tommy pushed forward and leaned against Beth Ann's shoulder. "It's okay,

Lady Bee. People say bad things, but they don't know us. Not the real us."

"Who told you that?" Robert asked.

"Dougie."

Beth Ann shifted her gaze to the older boy. He looked away, but she couldn't mistake the tight line of his lips. How many insults had he or his siblings endured?

"Some people don't realize how much words can hurt," she said.

"Some people do!" Dougie spat the words, then hurried to apologize. "I'm not mad at you, Lady Bee."

"I know you're not." She stood and let her gaze travel from one beloved face to the next, from Crystal to Tommy to Dougie. "If someone says something nasty to you, come to me."

The younger two agreed, but Dougie said, "I'm not going to let anyone abuse my brother and sister and do nothing."

"I'm not talking about doing nothing." She couldn't fail to notice how Robert's shoulders grew taut and his fingers closed into fists.

Had she said something to distress him? Had Dougie? She replayed the words in her mind, and she guessed at least one had upset him. Though she wanted to ask which, she couldn't in front of the children.

Forcing another smile, she tried to keep her voice cheerful as she asked, "How about some Christmas pie?"

"What's Christmas pie?" Crystal asked, stuffing the tissue in her pocket.

"Pie you eat at Christmas," grumbled her older brother.

Paying Dougie no mind, because she suspected he wanted to start another argument in order to release the strong emotions swirling inside him, Beth Ann said, "Your brother is right."

Dougie pasted on a superior grin.

It faded when Beth Ann added, "And your brother is wrong."

"It's not Christmas yet," Crystal argued. "How can we have Christmas pie?"

"Because it's the Christmas season. Remember how a candle was lit in church on Sunday to commemorate the beginning of

Advent? This is the time of year when we anticipate celebrating the wondrous gift God gave us when He sent His son to be born as a little baby on a special night."

Robert matched her smile as they moved out of the mill and toward the bridge and the diner on its far side. "So what's Christmas pie? Is it a tradition you had in your family?"

"Yes. We had mincemeat pie during Advent."

"Meat in pie?" Crystal's nose wrinkled. "Ugh!"

"In this case, the meats are those of fruits, especially apples and raisins."

"Why don't they call it minced apple and raisin pie?" asked the ever-practical Tommy.

"A good question," she answered. "I don't know. Do you, Robert?"

"The plainest Amish put beef in their mincemeat pie." He chuckled, and she knew her face had betrayed her. "Does that mean you've tried it?"

"I love mincemeat pie. The kind with

fruits and spices. So when I was offered a piece after one birth, I took a big eager bite." She grimaced again. "It had beef in it. I swallowed it as fast as I could to get the taste out of my mouth. The family thought I loved the pie, so they made sure there was a large piece waiting for me whenever I came to the house for a checkup or birth."

As he laughed, the children rushed ahead to stop in the middle of the bridge's span to stare at the brook that gurgled over the stones. The light from the waning full moon frosted the tips of each tiny wave. Dougie looked over the top of the concrete railing, but Crystal and Tommy peered through the openings at the water below them.

Robert chuckled beside her. "So let me guess. You ate the old-fashioned mincemeat every time without complaint."

"I did." She laughed. "Well, without complaining out loud."

"You don't ever complain."

"Not out loud."

He shook his head. "You don't ever complain. You take care of someone else's *kinder* without hesitation, and you're giving them a home they haven't had in who knows how long."

"Trust me. There was plenty of hesitation on my part."

"I do trust you."

Her breath caught at the undercurrent of emotion in his simple answer. "I'm glad to hear that. I got a message from their social worker this afternoon. She was supposed to come tomorrow, which is why I stayed home today to make sure everything was as perfect as possible before her visit."

"I wondered why you didn't come to the project house today."

"That's why, but now her visit is going to be the day after tomorrow. She promised me she wouldn't put off the visit again."

"Gut."

"Good? What if she decides to take the children and place them in other homes? What if they can't be together?"

He paused and faced her. "Why are you looking for trouble? God brought you to the *kinder.* He knows what lies before them and before you. Trust *Him.*"

"I try to." She gave him a wry grin. "It's just...just..."

"They've become important to you?"

She nodded, not trusting her voice to speak. The idea of the three youngsters being separated in the foster care system frightened her, because she wasn't sure what they might do to get back together. Nobody had told her how much longer their mother would be in rehab. When she got out, would she be able to care for her children?

"Don't forget," he murmured, "as important as they are to you, they're even more important to God." His smile returned. "How about getting some Christmas pie before we have to fish three *kinder* out of the brook?"

With a yelp, she rushed forward to keep Crystal from hoisting Tommy to see over the rail. Robert was right. She needed to enjoy the children while she could. She wished she could forget how he'd reacted with what appeared to be barely suppressed anger in the mill. She needed to find a way to ask him, but some sense she couldn't name warned her to be cautious in choosing her words.

Very cautious.

Chapter Nine

"Robert, I need to talk to you *now*."

Lowering his hammer, Robert was startled by the tremor in Beth Ann's voice as she wove among the volunteers to come to where he stood beside the unbroken window in the bedroom. He'd been given the task of putting up the molding around the windows. The other one was covered with plywood, but he'd be able to set the molding in place when he finished with this window.

"I'm listening," he said as he positioned another nail.

She lowered her voice as she came to stand beside him. "We've got a problem. A big problem."

He didn't hit the nail as he looked at Beth Ann's pale face. "Are the *kinder* okay?" He shoved his hammer into the loop on his belt. Letting the piece of molding slide to the floor, he resisted the urge to put his arm around her.

Something must be wrong. Really wrong.

"They're okay, but…" She took a deep breath. "It's Dougie. He's gotten into trouble at school."

"What kind of trouble?" He was amazed he had to coax each syllable out of her.

"A fight."

"A fight?" *Please, Lord, let it have been a battle of words.*

His prayer came too late because she answered, "A fistfight. He's not badly hurt. He may have a black eye, but his nose isn't broken."

"The other *kind*?"

"He's going to have two black eyes, and his nose is definitely broken."

"Can you take Dougie to the *doktor* without the social worker's okay?"

"I put ice on his eye." She wrung her

hands. "I'm not as worried about the social worker showing up tomorrow as I am about what led to the fight."

He nodded. Though the social worker might be very upset, DCF must be grateful Beth Ann had taken on the huge task of caring for the three *kinder*.

She wrapped her arms around herself and shifted from one foot to the other. Not because she was cold, he guessed, though the day was damp and raw. She was so distressed she couldn't conceal her anxiety.

"What made Dougie punch the other kid?" he asked.

"Why are you assuming he swung first?"

"He hurt the other boy more. I doubt he would have done as much damage if the other kid had hit him first." He gave her a swift smile. "I may be Amish, but I was also a boy, and we learned that lesson from other plain *kinder* and from our *Englisch* friends."

Her taut shoulders eased. "True. You may want to be separate from the rest of the world, but it intrudes, doesn't it?" Without giving him a chance to answer, she continued, "The other boy—his name's Aiden Bryson. He's been taunting Dougie every day for the past week."

"Taunting? What's he been saying?"

She shook her head. "Suffice it to say Aiden kept after Dougie about every aspect of his life, his family and his clothes until Dougie couldn't stand it. I don't think it's the first time he's had to put up with other kids picking on him or Crystal. That may be why he was reluctant to return to school and why he stopped going in the first place."

Robert knew how much words could hurt. *Nearly as much as my* daed*'s hand*, he thought before he could halt himself. It hadn't taken his *daed* long to go from calm to lashing out at him or one of his siblings. Dougie was a *kind*, so to expect the boy to endure such insulting provocation day after day might have been too much to ask.

Beth Ann's eyes filled with tears. "He never gave me a clue about what he was suffering, Robert. He thinks he can handle anything, but he can't. Not alone. If he won't trust me enough to tell me about being bullied, how can I protect him?"

"If you talk to him…"

"I don't think that will do any good in the short time we may have."

"Short time? What do you mean?"

"The school said if he gets into another fight, he'll be suspended. Both he and Crystal are behind their classmates. If he's kicked out for three days, it could be enough to keep him from moving ahead with his class in the spring."

Robert rubbed his fingers over his chin. It was clean-shaven. He shouldn't have to deal with the problems of parenting when he'd never grown a beard to show his married status.

He shook away his selfish thoughts. Beth Ann hadn't asked for these problems when she offered to take supper to hungry *kinder.*

Inspiration burst into his brain. "Have you considered homeschooling?"

"Homeschooling?" she repeated. "Do you have the time to do that?"

It was his turn to be shocked. "I assumed… That is, I… No, I don't have time. Do you?"

"I could, but where? The apartment isn't big enough. I can't imagine them getting much done if Tommy is trying to convince them to play with him."

"Everything okay?" asked Michael as he stuck his head past the door. His smile vanished as he walked in. "I can see that it isn't."

Beth Ann gave him a quick recap, finishing with, "We're discussing if I should remove the children from school and homeschool them."

Michael leaned his elbow on the rung of a ladder. "Cora is homeschooling our kids, though we hope, next year, to build a schoolhouse on the piece of land Isaac has donated."

"Would she be willing to take two more *kinder* to homeschool?" asked Robert.

"The Henderson *kinder* are *Englisch*. I don't know if they'd be allowed to have an Amish teacher."

"That could be checked with the public school," Beth Ann said. "And with their social worker, who's coming tomorrow."

"Sounds like a *gut* idea." Michael glanced at Robert, who nodded in agreement. "The *kinder* will understand you're trying to do what's best for them. Remember, it may have been a long time since they've had an adult who's ready to step forward to advocate for them."

"I want to change that," she replied.

Robert said, "So do I."

Beth Ann had planned to keep the children home the next day. Dougie and Crystal were thrilled to play hooky, but Tommy was annoyed because the day care kids were working on ornaments to be shared with the residents of a nursing home on the west side of Evergreen Corners. She gave each of the older two a book to read and cautioned them not to touch anything in the kitchen while she took Tommy to the church to join his friends in Gwen's class.

The anxiety that had kept her awake

continued to flicker through her head as she and Tommy crossed the village green. Someone had been working on the gazebo, repairing the damage left by the flood. The repair probably had been done by an Amish volunteer, seeing a problem and taking care of it.

That was what the plain community did, both Mennonite and Amish. Yet there seemed to be a tighter sense of belonging among the Amish than she'd known growing up Mennonite.

Maybe they acted like one big family, she thought to distract herself from her roiling thoughts, *because so many are related to one another*.

It was impossible for her to ignore how, when she and Robert had been discussing the problem Dougie was having at school, Michael had stepped in with a quick and reasonable solution. Unlike *Englischers* would have, Michael hadn't said he had to check with his wife. He'd known she, like anyone else in the Amish community, would agree in order to help someone in need.

She sighed as she and Tommy reached the church. Going downstairs with him, she gave Gwen a smile and told them both to have a nice day. She hurried away before she could be drawn into a conversation. She was too perplexed by her own thoughts to pay attention to anyone else's.

Heading toward the green again, she wondered how it would be to live Amish. No Amish person ever had to feel lonely as she had after her grandmother died and the clinic closed. Every event in an Amish life happened among family and friends. Births, marriages, deaths. Each brought everyone together. It was a well-ordered life, nothing like the chaos of her own.

She only had to look as far as Robert. He'd been separated from his sister for two decades, but she'd welcomed him back into her life and inspired him to be part of Amish Helping Hands. Neither of them acted as if their actions were anything out of the ordinary.

They weren't for the Amish.

"Hey!" came a shout an instant before

a strong arm swept around her arm and pulled her backward.

The leap of her heart told her the arm belonged to Robert. Before she could ask why he was grabbing her, she saw a car race past her, less than a foot away. She backed up and bumped into the hard wall of his chest.

Sensations exploded through her, wiping her mind clear of anything but the thought of his strength surrounding her. Bouncing in her chest, her heart urged her to soften against him as she savored the cool, fresh smell of him. She knew if she looked past the brim of her bonnet, she'd see his hair was damp from his morning shower.

She didn't move. She relished being in his arms while everything seemed to be as it was meant to be.

He shifted, and the moment was gone. She bit back a soft sigh of sorrow.

Robert readjusted the straps of a burlap bag hanging over his shoulder. "You almost walked in front of that car, you know. What were you thinking?"

She fought her fingers, which wanted to

reach up and rest on the buttons of his coat. Keeping them clenched at her sides, she imagined how he'd react if she shared the thoughts weighing on her heart. Thoughts of her future she couldn't imagine. The children's futures were more up in the air than hers. They had a mother, and it would be best for them to be returned to Kim when she finished with rehab.

Wouldn't it? What if Kim began using drugs again? What would happen to Dougie, Crystal and Tommy then? Would anyone be there for the children, or would they be left on their own all over again?

Nothing was simple or straightforward any longer.

Beth Ann stepped away, hoping she'd be able to think more clearly if she wasn't wrapped in his embrace. His fingers cupped her elbows, and she couldn't move farther without jerking herself out of his hands. She knew she should, but she didn't. She raised her eyes to meet his and saw strong emotions within them. That astonished her, because he seldom revealed his thoughts, but she realized he'd been deeply frightened by her carelessness.

Knowing he deserved an answer to his question, she said, "I guess I was lost in my thoughts."

"You need to be more careful. What would have happened to the Henderson *kinder* if you ended up in the hospital or worse?"

"I guess you would have become their sole temporary guardian." She meant her words to be teasing, but knew she'd failed when his eyes narrowed.

"This isn't a joke, Beth Ann. Don't you realize how important you are to—?" He coughed hard. "Don't you realize how important you are to them? Without you, they'll be sent to separate foster homes."

She nodded as she wished she could be sure she'd heard what she thought she had. Had he been about to include himself in the question about her being an important part of their lives? Had his cough been a way to disguise his near slip?

Her heart pleaded with her to ask, but

she didn't. Instead, she apologized. He was such a private man, and if she put him on the spot, she could ruin their friendship. She wasn't willing to risk that, not even for her heart's sweetest longings.

"I kept the children home from school today," Beth Ann said to change the subject. "Tommy wanted to go to day care, so I took him to the church."

He rubbed his hands on his trousers. "You left the other two alone?"

"With books to read."

His face altered with his grin. "You expect Dougie Henderson to sit and read? This, I've got to see."

"Come on." She motioned up the hill toward the apartment.

The walk went quickly because Robert told funny stories about his nieces' attempt to convince the kitten to hunt mice that had taken up residence in the old farmhouse for the winter. Laughing, she pushed aside her darker thoughts of what she had to tell him after her call with the social worker early that morning. He wasn't going to like what she had to say, and she wasn't sure how to break that news to him.

When she opened the door at the top of the stairs, Beth Ann wasn't surprised to see both kids raise their books in front of their faces.

"It might be more plausible to believe you'd actually been reading," she said as she took off her coat and hung it in the closet, "if your book wasn't upside down, Dougie."

"Oops." He gave her and Robert a lop-sided grin.

She returned it, not eager to get into a long debate with him.

Crystal jumped off the sofa and ran to fling her arms around Robert. He looked surprised and pleased at the same time as she shot a dozen questions at him, not giving him a chance to answer even.

When she paused to take a breath, he said, "I'll answer your last question first. I'm here because it's time for Dougie to start learning to drive a buggy."

"You're teaching me to drive? Today?"

A rare, genuine smile brightened the boy's face, which was already rounder than it'd been the evening Beth Ann had first taken him into the community center.

"If you'd like."

"If I...?" He let out a whoop. "Let's go." He pushed past Beth Ann to yank his coat out of the closet. "Is it okay, Lady Bee?"

"Yes, if you promise to listen to everything Robert tells you and you'll do as he says."

"Don't I always?"

"No," she replied at the same time Robert did.

"I will today. I promise." He ran to look out the window. "Hey, where's the horse and buggy?"

Robert shrugged off his coat and reached into the bag he'd had over his shoulder. He pulled out a pair of long leather straps. "Before you drive a horse, you need to learn how to hold the reins."

Dougie grabbed the ends, raising them and slapping hard. "Like that, right?"

"Wrong." Robert took the reins from the

boy. "*Komm* and sit. I'll show you. Beth Ann, will you be our horse?"

"All right." She took one end of the reins and moved toward the kitchen door as he instructed. Turning so she could watch, she leaned one shoulder against the door molding.

Dougie sat on one side of Robert, and Crystal was perched on the other. Both children swung their feet, unable to restrain their excitement.

"Take one rein in each hand, Dougie," Robert said. "Hold the reins between your thumb and the first finger." He smiled when the boy grasped the leather straps as he'd instructed. "*Gut!* Let the reins drop across your palm and out through the space between your last two fingers."

Dougie followed the instructions with his right hand, but struggled to make the strap in his left hand do as he wished. Again and again, he tried to slip it between his fingers and missed.

Robert started to reach out to help him, but Crystal said, "Start with your left hand first, Dougie, then grasp the right rein."

The boy managed to get the grip on his first try. "I did it!"

Beth Ann and his sister cheered. They laughed when Dougie reminded Beth Ann she was supposed to be the horse. Next, Crystal was given her chance to hold the reins. It took the girl more time to get her fingers to cooperate, but soon the children were able to grasp the reins correctly. They protested when Robert said the lesson was over for that day.

"You'll be driving a buggy sooner than you think," Robert said. "Don't be discouraged that it takes time. A horse isn't like a car. It's a living, breathing creature. You want to know *everything* about the best way to treat the horse before you handle a real one." He smiled. "Of course, that means spending time with Clipper, so he gets to know everything about you, too."

The children's faces glowed, and they both began to talk at the same time as they went into the bedroom to pick up the toys they'd gotten out while she was taking their little brother to the church.

She rolled the straps up as she walked to the sofa. "I want to thank you, too. They loved that lesson."

Robert stood, his eyes twinkling. "Don't you want to learn to drive?"

"I guess so." She laughed. "As long as you don't laugh at me. I tried once before. A group of young children thought it would be great fun to teach someone as old as me. I've got to tell you I didn't learn much because the kids were too busy watching the horse lead the buggy where it wanted to go instead of where I did."

"You've learned the first lesson. You have to be in charge, not the horse."

"I'll keep that in mind," she replied, trying to sound nonchalant. "When you take the children out in the buggy, I could go along and take my turn."

"Or come along without them."

She started to reply, then was halted by the warmth in his eyes. Was he asking her to join him in his borrowed buggy as if it were his courting buggy and he was taking her home from a youth event? Neither of them were youths any longer, and she must be mistaken. Robert must select an Amish woman for his wife. Not a Mennonite who was on the fence about her future.

Hating how she had to answer him, but telling herself it was for the best as his gaze lost its sparkle, she said, "Let's see what happens, okay? Everything could change after the social worker comes."

"True."

"I need to make sure I ask her about taking Tommy to the doctor to see what they can do for his slap step. It may mean him wearing a brace like mine. I hope it won't make him stick out as mine did when I was a kid." She bit back her bitterness that the brace had made her even more of a pariah when she was an adult.

"We each bear scars gathered during our lives. Some are visible. Some aren't. However, we're loved in God's eyes, and that's what is important."

"It's easy to say, but the real world isn't like that. People stare and act as if I'm somehow deficient because I wear a brace.

I don't want Tommy to feel that way, but it's important he gets help or his uneven steps will become more pronounced as he grows."

He put his hand close to hers on the reins, not touching, but she was as aware of every inch of him as if he had wrapped her hand in his. A warmth sizzled across her skin while she fought her sudden desire to reach out and entwine her fingers with his.

In the gentlest tone she'd ever heard him use, he said, "If he ends up wearing a brace, Tommy will have you as a model for how to handle any comments. I know you'll help him see how important it is for each of us to care for one another, no matter what we can do or what we can't. Tommy is God's beloved *kind*."

"It may be irrelevant if the social worker doesn't agree for me to take him to the doctor."

"What time is she coming? I'll be here."

She looked away, knowing the moment she had dreaded had arrived. Oh, how she wished she could have avoided it, because she knew what she was about to say would hurt him. Quietly, keeping her eyes averted, she said, "She told me that, as the children are living with me, I'm the only one she wants to meet with on this visit."

"But you explained that I'm helping with the *kinder*, too, ain't so?"

"I did, but she was insistent."

"So you gave in."

That he didn't make it a question revealed how deeply he was wounded by being left out of the discussion about the children's futures.

"I tried to convince her," she said. "I really tried, but she said for this first visit, she wanted only to talk to me and the kids."

His face became a blank mask. "All right. As you don't need me..." He took the reins, pulled his coat on and set his hat on his head.

He was waiting for her to say something, but she didn't know how to reply.

When the door closed behind him, Beth Ann feared she'd made the biggest mistake of her life.

Chapter Ten

Everything went well the next morning, in spite of Beth Ann's anxiety about the upcoming meeting. It might have been easier if she'd gotten a decent night's sleep. Too many thoughts had played through her head all night, scenarios where she'd found the right thing to say so Robert wouldn't have stormed out. Each one of them ended the same way, with him walking out without even looking back at her.

Those thoughts made her steps ponderous while she got the children ready for the social worker's visit. Even Tommy, who was impatient to return to his friends at the day care center, seemed to understand he needed to cooperate. She suspected Dougie had had a talk with his younger siblings the previous evening when she was cleaning up the kitchen after a meal everyone agreed wasn't as bad as her earlier efforts at cooking. Though she wanted to thank him, she didn't. Dougie might have figured she owed him a favor for his assistance.

Beth Ann made sure every surface in the apartment was clean and uncluttered. She did the same with the children, sending Dougie into the bedroom to change into jeans that didn't have patches on the knees. Tommy wanted to wear the paper snowman hat he'd made earlier in the week, and she relented, deciding it was better to let him look silly than to have his face blotched with tears.

The apartment smelled of lemon cleaner and fresh lemon bars Gladys had brought for Beth Ann to serve to the social worker. Pacing as she watched the street for an unfamiliar car to stop in front of the driveway, Beth Ann tried to make her stomach relax. It was impossible.

How she wished Robert could have been there with her! Maybe she should have tried harder to convince the social worker that she and Robert were equal partners in raising the children. Yet she'd feared if she'd pushed too much the social worker would label her difficult and insist on taking the kids today. What a conundrum with no solution! Choosing between Robert's feelings and the children's best interests was almost impossible, but she had. Now he was hurt, and she was unsure if she could find a way to apologize.

After her preparations and reminders to the children to be on their best behavior, the visit from Deana Etheridge was anticlimactic. The harried social worker had been kind, but in an obvious hurry. She wanted to see where the children slept and spoke to them briefly before asking if they could wait somewhere out of earshot.

Beth Ann was glad when Tony Whittaker, the mayor's husband, quickly agreed to watch the children. Her friends in Evergreen Corners were eager to do whatever they could to make sure the meeting went well. The children left with Tony, who was gracious and welcoming to Deana while managing to compliment Beth Ann for how well she cared for them.

Hoping she wasn't blushing at the un-expected testimonial, Beth Ann answered each of the social worker's questions. She said nothing about her plans to have Dougie and Crystal homeschooled, but offered to take Deana to see Tommy's day care center.

The social worker thanked her but de-murred before adding, "These matters will be of more concern when they have their foster placement. As this is a temporary situation, I'm more interested they're in a safe environment." She closed her com-puter where she'd been taking notes, un-aware of how her assumption the children would soon be in foster care chilled Beth Ann to the marrow. "I hope you realize how unusual this situation is. If my boss hadn't been so familiar with your pastor, I'm sure nobody would have okayed this placement."

"I feel blessed to have them in my life."

"Would you be interested in becoming a licensed foster parent?" She collected the sheaf of papers Beth Ann had signed and handed back the ones that would allow her to take the children to the doctor. "I can have the application paperwork mailed to you."

"If I do, could I keep Dougie, Crystal and Tommy?"

She shook her head. "I'm sorry, but they'll need to be settled before you can be licensed." Coming to her feet, she smiled what looked like a genuine smile for the first time. "I'm sorry, Ms. Overholt. It's clear you've done a wonderful thing by taking these children in, but we've bent the rules as much as we can."

"Can you tell me if they'll be placed in the same home?"

"I wish I could, but that'll depend on if there are foster parents who can take three children at once." She picked up her purse and flung the strap over her shoulder. "We don't have a lot of people willing or able to take three."

"The children need to remain together."

"We try to arrange for siblings to see each other whenever possible."

"They depend on one another."

"Don't you see, Ms. Overholt? Children shouldn't have to depend on each other. They should have dependable adults in their lives, so they can be children."

Knowing she was fighting a bureaucratic battle she couldn't win, she asked, "How long do you think they'll be able to stay?" She stumbled to her feet, numb. She hadn't realized how much she'd dared to believe the kids would be allowed to remain with her.

"We won't move them before year's end. If you want to prepare them, I'd say a good guesstimate would be around mid-January."

A little over a month from now? She must have said something polite as the social worker left, saying she'd return on Christmas Eve to start the work to move the children into foster care. The words resonated through Beth Ann's skull, leaving it aching and as heavy as her heart. Looking around the room, she saw signs of the children everywhere. Dougie's pillow on the sofa. Crystal's missing barrette. Tommy's beloved stuffed bear.

She collapsed into the chair at the table and covered her face with her hands. *God, I know I've asked for so much in the past year. Forget everything else I've asked for. Please send me help to save these children from being taken away and separated. Please!*

Clouds were thickening overhead when Beth Ann decided to leave the apartment much later that afternoon. Tony had stopped by after Deana departed to let her know he'd delivered the older kids to the Millers, who would take them to the community center at supper time, and Tommy to day care. The mayor's husband didn't ask about the meeting with the social worker. Beth Ann's expression must have told him it hadn't gone the way she'd hoped.

As soon as she was confident she could speak without sobbing, Beth Ann had made an appointment for the next day with Dr. Kingsley's office to take the children in for a checkup. She'd waited for Robert to come to the apartment, but he hadn't. She'd assumed he'd show up as soon as he'd heard Deana had left, because he'd been as nervous about the meeting as she'd been. Or he had been before she'd told him Deana didn't want to talk to him at the first meeting. Had his feelings been so hurt that he'd washed his hands of the whole situation?

No, he was peeved with her, but he cared about the children and wanted to make sure they were kept together. Something important must have been keeping him busy. Her stomach clenched as she wondered if he'd been distracted by a job interview. She should wish him the best, because it was important for him to find a paying job so he could remain in Evergreen Corners with his sister. Yet she wanted to talk to him about what had occurred and get his take on what to do next to protect the kids. She hadn't realized how much of a team they'd become, the five of them, but that wouldn't last unless they found a way to convince DCF to change its collective mind.

The problem was they weren't a real family. The children had a mother, and Beth Ann and Robert were friends, not a married couple. In DCF's eyes, they had nothing to offer the children.

"Other than love and nurturing and a faith-filled home," she said aloud while she buttoned her coat.

With a sigh as she tied on her bonnet, she knew she needed to look for a job herself. The money she'd saved was almost gone, as were the funds from Pastor Hershey. If bags of groceries hadn't been turning up outside the apartment door, she would have been broke already.

As the wind pulled at her scarf, she bent her head into its iciness. She kept one hand on her bonnet. She wondered if it had ever taken longer to cross the green. When she heard the church bell peal five times, she sighed. There was no sense going to the project house this late in the day. The team would be cleaning up and heading home soon, so she wouldn't find Robert there.

Deciding to get the children a treat because they'd been so good, she headed toward the general store across from the brook. The kids liked coconut bars. She'd get a few and pick up Tommy before going to the community center to meet the older two.

The store was empty when she went in. It had been established, according to a sign on its front porch, more than 150 years before. Inside, other than electric lights and a cooler holding soda, juice and milk, it didn't look as if it had been changed since the day it opened. Dark beams ran overhead, and the floor under her feet had been stripped of any polish long ago by muddy boots and dirty shoes.

"I'm Mrs. Weiskopf," announced a voice from the far end of the store, where a large counter held an antique cash register. The white-haired woman there resembled pictures Beth Ann had seen of Mrs. Claus.

"How can I help you?" Her eyes narrowed. "Hey, aren't you Beth Ann Overholt?"

"I am." She didn't need to ask how Mrs. Weiskopf had recognized her. Most people began any description of her with the brace she wore.

Mrs. Weiskopf smiled. "I thought I recognized you from when you came in with the Henderson children before Thanksgiving and let them pick out some candy. It's a good thing you're doing to help those kids. None of us realized how horrific that place of theirs was. Their aunt kept saying she was getting someone to clear it out." Her lips pursed. "Nobody guessed she'd start by clearing herself out of town."

"She might come back."

Mrs. Weiskopf sniffed her disagreement before adding, "It'd be better if she stayed away and let good souls like you and your boyfriend take care of the kids."

"Robert isn't—" She halted herself when she realized debating the issue could add to the gossip floating through Evergreen

Corners. "Robert isn't going to stand to one side and do nothing."

"Nor will you, as we've seen." The white-haired woman threw her hands in the air. "I shouldn't either. I've waited too long to tell you a letter arrived for you this morning. A certified letter." She rolled her eyes as if she were no older than Crystal. "I should have mentioned it as soon as you came in. My mind can't keep track of details like it used to." She sighed. "I used to look forward to coming in every day."

She walked away so Beth Ann didn't have a chance to respond. When she returned, she put a business-sized envelope on the counter. It had a card attached to the top, which she deftly removed.

"Sorry to be complaining," she said. "My sister called from Florida this morning and told me how nice and warm it is. She's been trying to get me to move down there since my husband died five years ago. On days like this when the cold gnaws at my bones, I'm ready to agree." She pushed the card toward Beth Ann and handed her a pen. "You need to sign and date this."

She did, and the older woman handed her the letter. She didn't recognize the names on the return address, but her eyes widened when she saw "Attorneys-at-Law" on the next line. Why would a lawyer be sending her a certified letter?

Knowing the answer would have to wait, she bought a half dozen candy bars for the children. She'd give them each one tonight and save the others for another special occasion.

Don't save them too long, because they may not be here much longer.

She ignored the annoying voice in her head, thanked Mrs. Weiskopf, who handed her the bag with the candy and her change, and headed out of the store. She got only as far as the front porch before she couldn't stand the suspense any longer. Shoving the candy into her pocket, she opened the letter.

She drew in a sharp gasp. Her aunt, Helen Friesen, had died two months ago in California. The lawyers had been searching for

Helen's family and discovered Beth Ann's address.

Beth Ann groped for a seat on the bench beside the door as she continued reading. She was her aunt's sole heir, and the lawyers needed her to contact them so her aunt's estate could be turned over to her. It was... She turned the page and stared at the figure at the bottom of long rows of columns.

$383,810.27

More than a *quarter million* dollars! It was enough money for her to live on, if she was frugal, for years. She wouldn't need to worry about keeping the kids fed if they remained with her far longer than Deana had led her to believe. Or she could buy a nice home and land in Evergreen Corners. Or she could go to college and get her nursing degree, something she'd longed to do when she was a little girl.

Her eyes widened further when she saw the money had been left to her with the stipulation that she spend the money to make herself happy.

Your aunt stated she wished she could have spent time with you, helping you make your dreams come true. This is the way she can ensure that can happen.

Her dreams come true? A hysterical laugh tickled her throat. The money couldn't guarantee the children would remain together or with her. She realized with a soft hiccup of sadness, it couldn't change her heart, which wanted to belong to Robert Yoder, though he'd never select a wife who wasn't Amish.

Unable to halt her tears, she looked at the very bottom of the letter. It concluded with a request for her to contact the office as soon as possible.

She pulled her cell phone out of her purse. Her fingers shook so much she misdialed three times. When an answering machine asked her to leave her name, phone number and reason for calling, she almost hung up.

Somehow, she managed to say, "I'm Beth Ann Overholt. I received a letter today about my aunt's estate." She gave her phone number and hoped she'd gotten the digits in the right order. Her thoughts were jumping around like water on a hot greased griddle, and she couldn't grasp a single one.

Ending the call, she sat and stared at the screen, unable to believe such a windfall was hers.

What was she going to do with it?

Robert paused in front of the store when he saw Beth Ann hunched on the bench on the porch. The three *kinder* stopped, too, their eyes wide.

She held something in her hand. Her phone, he realized. She looked as if she'd been beaten.

At the thought, he shuddered. He knew what it looked like when someone he cared about had suffered vicious blows. Nobody would have struck Beth Ann. Not literally. Another shiver cut through him. Had the meeting gone so poorly with the social worker?

"Beth Ann?"

Her head jerked up, and she rubbed both cheeks in an effort to hide the trails left by her grief. Standing, she stuffed some paper and her phone into her purse. Did she think he'd buy the fake smile she pasted on her face?

"Just the people I wanted to see," she said as she descended to the sidewalk.

He didn't smile, and neither did the children.

"How did it go with the social worker?" he asked.

Before she could answer, a strange sound came from her purse. Her face blanched, and she said, "I've got to take this call. Excuse me."

He watched as she hurried onto the porch as if a wolf nipped at her heels. She paused by the door and spoke too low for him to hear.

"Is Beth Ann okay?" asked Tommy.

At the anxiety in the little boy's voice, Robert forced a smile. "She's fine. She just doesn't want to bother everyone with her conversation."

Dougie grimaced. "Or she doesn't want us to know she's talking to her boyfriend."

"We don't know who's calling her," he replied, trying not to let the boy's words bother him.

Listening to a ten-year-old's speculations was foolish. Beth Ann had never spoken of anyone special in Pennsylvania or in Evergreen Corners. The contrary side of his mind asked why she would talk about such personal matters with him when he was so careful never to speak of his past.

Beth Ann returned to where they stood. As if the phone hadn't rung and distracted her, she said, "You were asking about the social worker's visit." She smiled at the *kinder.* "Want the best news first? You're going to be staying with me for a while."

Tommy and Crystal grabbed each other's hands and jumped in a circle. They tried to get Dougie to join them, but he clasped his fingers behind him.

"What's the not-so-best other news?" he asked.

Her smile faltered.

Realizing she didn't want to discuss the rest of what had been discussed in front of the *kinder*, Robert looped one arm through hers and another through Crystal's. "I'm hungry. Let's eat."

"Let's go to the community center tonight," she replied as she took Tommy's hand. "Who wants a yummy meal?"

That brought cheers from the *kinder*. When Beth Ann asked him how his day had gone, Robert guessed she was curious why he hadn't come to discover what happened with the social worker's visit. He explained he and one of the *Englisch* volunteers had to go to Rutland because of a mixed-up order.

"Some of the doorknobs were brass and others polished nickel, and they need to match." He related how he'd had to deal with a hapless clerk and ended up searching through the store for the items they needed. He made the whole experience sound silly, and soon Beth Ann was laughing.

As they walked to the community center, he hoped she hadn't guessed he wasn't sharing everything. The manager of the store, Nick, had been impressed with Robert's organizational skills and his commitment to the project. Nick had kept him there, asking him questions about if he was looking for work and how Nick could contact him if a job became available.

Rutland was too far from Evergreen Corners, a ninety-minute drive on dry roads. In the winter with snow and ice, the commute would be longer. Leaving Evergreen Corners was something he didn't want to contemplate, but the simple truth was he needed a job. He needed to finish paying off his *daed*'s debts and earn enough to live on.

Beth Ann said something to him. He didn't catch her words, but he couldn't ignore how the brush of her gloved fingers on his sleeve sent sweet warmth through him. The scent of something as fresh as lilacs filled each breath he took, banishing the evening chill. He should have been grateful the *kinder* surrounded them, because he was overwhelmed by the yearning to pull her into his arms and taste her lips, which appeared soft and welcoming.

He'd been able to control his temper while he was in Evergreen Corners. Most of the time. He hadn't lashed out with closed fists as his *daed* had. Maybe his prayers had been answered. If he could be sure, it might be time for those driving lessons he wanted to give Beth Ann without the *kinder* acting as chaperones.

The thought of how he'd ask her filled his mind, so he hardly tasted the roast beef with rich brown gravy splashed over buttery mashed potatoes. Only when Dougie announced he wanted to join the youth choir at the church where Tommy's day care was located did he chide himself for letting his imagination get in the way of his responsibilities. He couldn't become like his *mamm*, either, and pretend nothing was wrong when her *kinder* had been bruised by her husband's hand.

"A choir?" Beth Ann asked.

"Dougie likes to sing," Tommy said, thrilled to know something she didn't.

"I sang in it last year." The older boy raised his chin, ready to argue.

She must have seen his motion, too, because she said, "As long as you keep up your schoolwork and don't get into trouble, Dougie, I don't see why you can't sing in the choir again this year."

"Any trouble at all?" he asked.

"Any *big* trouble." She raised a single finger. "Don't ask me to define that. You know the answer as well as I do. Behave yourself, and you can have a good time with the choir."

He quickly nodded. He must have been eager to rejoin the choir if he was willing to comply with her rules.

"I want to sing, too," Crystal said. "I'm old enough this year."

"As long as you agree to the same rules Dougie has," Beth Ann replied with a smile as she glanced at Dougie. Did she expect him to protest his sister's participation?

The boy remained silent as his sister agreed.

Beth Ann turned the conversation to what she'd discussed with Deana Etheridge. Robert suspected she didn't reveal everything, because shadows clung to the corners of her eyes as she smiled while she told them about the stack of paperwork she had to read and sign.

"As I told you," she said, "the good news is you'll be staying with me through the holidays."

"After that?" asked Crystal.

"Let's put our faith in God's plan for us," Robert said. "Guessing won't get us anywhere. Besides, it's time to enjoy delicious brownies."

The *kinder* were distracted as they each reached for one on the plate in the center of the table. Dougie tried to sneak two, but set one back on the plate when Beth Ann frowned. The boy might not be learning manners. However, he'd discovered it was better to behave around Beth Ann.

Robert curbed his own impatience until the youngsters had finished and were handing their dirty dishes to a volunteer. He watched them join other kids playing with a box of toys at the rear of the community center.

"I'm sorry," Beth Ann said, and he turned back to her.

"About what?"

"Last night. You're right. I should have insisted that Deana talk to both of us, but I was worried that if I pushed too hard, she'd take the kids today."

He nodded. "I figured that out on my way home when I cooled off. So how did it go? Really?"

He listened when she shared with him all that had been said during the short visit, her bright green eyes glimmering with tears. He didn't care that they were sitting in the community center. He reached over and put his much larger hand over her trembling fingers.

"We'll talk to Pastor Hershey," he said. "Maybe he can do something."

"Maybe." She didn't add anything more, and he heard the depth of her discouragement in that single word.

He waited, but she remained silent. Knowing one of the *kinder* could trot up at any moment with a question or to show off something they'd created out of the box of old toys, he asked, "What was all that secrecy at the store when you got a call?"

"It's been an odd day," she said.

"Odd?" He hadn't expected her to say that. "In what way?"

She hesitated, then drew her hand out from beneath his. Dropping it to her lap, she sighed. "I'd just found out my aunt has died in California. She made me her sole heir."

"Do you have to go there to settle her estate?" He was astonished at the intensity of his hope she wouldn't be leaving Evergreen Corners. She had become such a vital part of his life in the past few weeks, and he had a difficult time thinking of her being so far away.

"No, there are lawyers handling it." She gnawed on her lower lip. "She's left me a large sum of money." She hesitated before telling him the amount along with the limits her *aenti* had put on it.

"Beth Ann, that's *gut* news." Realizing how his words must have sounded, he hurried to add, "Not about your *aenti*'s death, but she must have loved you very much."

"How could she when she didn't know me? I never remember her coming to visit my grandmother and me."

"Maybe your *grossmammi* wrote to her about you often enough so your *aenti* felt she knew you. At least enough to make you her heir."

"I don't know, Robert." She looked at him for the first time since she'd mentioned her *aenti*. "I don't know what to think or what to do."

"You don't do anything other than pray and let God show you the way He wants you to go."

A faint smile pulled at her lips and at his heart. "Thank you, Robert. I needed to hear good advice. I should have known you'd be the one to offer it."

Her words made him feel something he hadn't in longer than he could remember. He felt he had done the right thing and didn't need to second-guess every word. Did she have any idea what a precious gift she'd given him? Probably not, but he wouldn't forget it.

Not ever.

Chapter Eleven

Beth Ann scooped up the towels on the bathroom floor and grimaced when she stepped into a puddle of water left. She'd insisted the children take baths before their visit to Dr. Kingsley's office, and the bathroom had been drenched.

"What's he going to do?" asked Crystal as she twisted her braids.

"He's going to look in your mouth and ask you to stick out your tongue." Beth Ann dropped the wet towels into the hamper. "He'll check your ears with a little light, and he'll listen to your heart."

"That's all?"

"Sometimes there are other things, but that's what a checkup means."

Tommy giggled. "Checkup! What a funny word! Check*up* my ears and *up* my mouth. Check*up* my nose?"

"Only if you've got a cold." Beth Ann couldn't keep from laughing. "You're healthy, so don't worry."

They rushed into the living room to share what they'd learned with Dougie. She knew they were hoping for the day when they'd discovered something he didn't know. They'd be waiting a long time, because if that happened, Dougie would never admit he hadn't known before they told him.

She made sure her own face was clean and her hair pulled beneath her *kapp* before she went out into the main room. About to ask if they were ready to go, she halted when she heard Tommy let out a soft squeal.

"They've got shots, pip-squeak," Dougie was saying.

"Shots?" The little boy's face blanched to the color of new snow.

"Yep. Long needles." Dougie put his hands a foot apart. "This long."

Beth Ann strode across the room. "Enough, Dougie. You need to stop picking on your little brother."

"Why? Isn't that what little brothers are for? To pick on?" He gave a terse laugh. "That's what Mom's buddy Striper said."

"Striper?" she asked.

Dougie refused to meet her eyes, and she guessed Striper had been someone involved with his mother's drug use.

A knock came at the door, and she opened it and greeted Robert. Soft flakes drifted around him, but there were four inches of new snow on the steps.

"Are you ready to go?" Snow fell off his clothes to melt around him. "It's brisk outside."

"It's not b-risk." Tommy wrapped his arms around himself. "It's *cold.*"

She clapped her hands. "Everyone, get your coats on. Don't forget your mittens and hats."

As the children rushed to obey, he said, "Sorry about the snow."

"Don't worry." She laughed. "Wait until you see how much three small pairs of feet can track in."

"You're amazing. Do you know that?"

"What's amazing about not worrying about things I can't do anything about? I'd rather be strong and know God is with me...including while cleaning up puddles on the floor."

He chuckled before gathering the children and opening the door. The boys hurried down the snowy steps, Tommy trying to keep up with his brother.

Beth Ann held her breath until the little boy reached the ground. She knew how precarious her own balance could be on the stairs, and she didn't want Tommy's visit to the doctor's office to start with him having a broken bone set.

Crystal paused on the landing, looking around. "There haven't been any groceries left in a while." She gave Beth Ann a worried glance.

She hugged the girl. "We've got plenty to eat." She shot a glance at Robert, which she hoped he understood meant he shouldn't say anything about her aunt's estate. She had no idea when she'd receive the money, but had been advised by her aunt's attorney to set up a bank account soon. "I know how you like Abby's brownies, Crystal."

That brought a smile to the girl's face, and she scurried to catch up with her brothers. Beth Ann followed at a more sedate pace with Robert behind her.

When they reached the green, the kids took off to run through the fresh snow. They chased each other and tossed snow into the air to blend with what was falling.

"I wonder how long they'll remain excited about the snow. Everyone else is complaining about how it arrived so early this year," Robert said.

"At their ages, I wouldn't have cared if it snowed year-round."

"Not me. I couldn't wait for spring so I could go fishing."

"You could try ice fishing."

He shook his head. "It hasn't been cold enough yet for the water to freeze enough to support me. By the time it does, who knows where I'll be?"

Her heart lurched as he spoke about leaving. "Have you given up on finding a job in Evergreen Corners?"

"Not yet."

"I know you want to work with wood."

Giving her a wry grin, he said, "I'd be willing to work at any place that would have me. You weren't at the project house yesterday when Michael said the rebuilding efforts would end by the first of February. Less than two months from now, and with the holidays in the middle, that's not a lot of time to find a job."

"Or a place to open your own shop."

"That is going to have to wait. I can't eat sawdust." He chuckled. "The electric company won't accept it as payment, either."

"Did you check?"

"Are you telling me I shouldn't give up?"

"You shouldn't. Not yet. You've got a

month and a half to make something happen. If anyone can do it, you can."

"I wish I had your faith."

"It doesn't matter what I feel you can do. It's what *you* feel you can do and what God has in store for you."

"*Danki*, Beth Ann, for reminding me of what I should already know."

"My pleasure."

"No." His voice took on a raspy edge. "No, it's *my* pleasure."

When he reached out and clasped her hand, she smiled up at him. The connection between them didn't need words. His fingers rose to cup her cheek, and the wintry cold vanished as she lost herself in his royal blue eyes and their invitation to step closer.

"Hey!" shouted Tommy. "Aren't you coming?"

Beth Ann blinked and saw Robert do the same. They'd been so wrapped up in the moment they'd forgotten where they were. Or at least she had. She drew her hand out of Robert's, and the full force of the cold wind struck her anew.

Neither of them spoke as they went to the doctor's office near the diner. When Robert opened the door and held it for them, she was conscious of how close they stood once again. She eased past him, making sure not even her coat brushed against him. If he touched her again, she doubted she could keep from throwing her arms around him.

The waiting room was full, but after Beth Ann checked with the clerk behind the half-glass reception wall, a woman moved to allow her to sit beside Robert. The three children went to sit on the floor with other youngsters watching cartoons.

Beth Ann looked up when a nurse called the children's names. She thought of the times she'd stepped into the clinic's waiting room to ask a patient to come in for an examination. A sharp pang cut through her, shocking her. Did she miss being a midwife that much? No, it wasn't being a midwife. What she missed was being able to step forward to help people who needed her skills and spending time with them, answering questions and soothing fears.

When Dougie whispered something in his brother's ear as they stood, Tommy squeaked with dismay. Beth Ann took Tommy's hand. She didn't need Dougie feeding Tommy more tales of fake horrors and torture he'd be facing in the examination room. However, she wasn't going to accuse Dougie in front of others when she had no proof other than his expression, which resembled a cat who'd swallowed a canary.

"Did you know, Tommy," she asked, "good boys get lollipops after they see the doctor?"

"Grape ones?"

She took a quick glance at the receptionist's desk and the glass jar holding a handful of treats. Seeing a couple of purple lollipops among the rainbow of colors, she said, "Yes, but we need to get in to see the doctor right away before someone else comes out and chooses them."

"Let's go." He gave her a grin so big it almost escaped his face.

Again they formed a parade with Beth Ann leading the way and Robert bringing up the rear. The nurse showed them to a room and told them the doctor would be in as soon as possible.

Robert stood by the sink while Beth Ann remained standing between Dougie and Tommy by the table. Crystal sat on one of the plastic chairs. They turned as a short, round man with gold-rimmed glasses perched on his bald head and a stethoscope dropping over his Patriots T-shirt walked in. He picked up a small computer from the counter near the sink and glanced at it.

Tommy asked, "When can I have my grape lollipop?"

"As soon as we're done, young fellow." The man introduced himself as Dr. Kingsley and asked for their names. "We've got the whole family, I see. Shall we get started?"

"May I speak with you first?" Beth Ann asked.

"Of course," he replied, though she could

see he was curious what they would talk about before he examined his patients.

She went into the hallway between the examination rooms. She waited until Dr. Kingsley had closed the door before she asked, "Could you examine Dougie and Crystal first?"

He looked at his handheld computer. "The older boy is Dougie, right?"

"Yes. Once you've examined them, Robert can take them into the waiting room while you check Tommy. I don't want to upset him by discussing his gait in front of his siblings."

"His slap gait."

Beth Ann relaxed a bit. "I should have guessed you'd notice it."

"Has he been in physical therapy for it?"

"I don't know. I don't know if he's ever seen a doctor for it."

Dr. Kingsley's brows arched. "You didn't know the children before you took them into your care?"

"I'd known them less than an hour." She explained how their mother was in rehab and they were staying with her through the holidays.

The doctor opened the door for her to re-enter the room. When he announced he'd start with the oldest, Tommy murmured about being afraid the grape lollipops would be gone before he was done. Robert calmed him by saying he'd make sure one was set aside for the boy.

The exams for the older two were done quickly. Beth Ann waited until Robert had steered them out before she put Tommy on the table. He started to protest, but she reminded him that Robert needed to make sure his grape lollipop was waiting for him.

Dr. Kingsley went through the same steps of checking Tommy's throat, his ears, and his heart and lungs. The little boy was fascinated when the doctor got out his small hammer to test his knee reflexes. While his left leg jerked, there wasn't much reaction from his right.

Lifting the little boy off the table, the doctor asked him to walk and to skip and hop with both feet striking at the same time.

Tommy couldn't do either, but the doctor's encouraging smile didn't waver.

"I wish all my patients were as good as you," the doctor said.

"You're not going to give me a shot, are you?" Tommy asked.

Dr. Kingsley chuckled. "I don't see any reason to give you a shot today." He glanced toward Beth Ann.

She didn't know if the children were up-to-date on their immunizations, so she shrugged.

He nodded, understanding what she hadn't said. When he turned the subject to Tommy's walking, the little boy listened. Dr. Kingsley wanted Tommy to start physical therapy at least once a week to strengthen his right leg muscles. In addition, he was going to contact DCF and get permission for the boy to be fitted with a brace.

Seeing Tommy's concern, he said, "Beth Ann will tell you it's a simple process. A technician puts plaster around your leg, the plaster like when someone breaks a leg. He'll remove it in a few minutes after it's dried. He'll use it to make a brace just for you."

"Like Beth Ann's?"

"Hers is plain white. You can have yours in another color if you want." He smiled. "The straps that hold it in place come in more colors."

Beth Ann thought he'd understood until Tommy announced as they emerged into the waiting room, "Guess what? The doctor's going to break my leg and give me a brace like Beth Ann's."

As the other patients turned to look at her, Beth Ann guessed her cheeks were red because heat was a thick aura around her. Telling herself nobody would take the little boy's words at face value didn't ease her embarrassment. She looked toward Robert who was trying to stifle a laugh, and she burst out with her own. She wished she could tell him how glad she was he'd come with them today.

While Beth Ann settled up with the receptionist, Robert oversaw the *kinder* putting on their coats. He wondered how she managed it multiple times each day because first one *kind*, then another needed help to get an arm down a sleeve or to find a mitten, or he had to referee a debate over which one had worn which hat to the *doktor*'s office. He fought his irritation when Dougie, for the second time, acted as if he'd lost his lollipop and was going to take either his sister's or brother's. He'd seen how the boy acted out when he felt circumstances were beyond his control, but the examination was done, so Dougie should be relieved.

They walked out onto the street with the *kinder* squabbling. He watched as Beth Ann regained some semblance of order by taking the younger two by the hands and insisting Dougie walk in front of her as they crossed the bridge and headed toward the green. Awed by her easy handling of the youngsters, he wondered what it would have been like to have had a parent who used a smile instead of the back of a hand.

In spite of his determination to keep his

focus on the *kinder*, Robert's gaze slipped to his left and the remnants of the covered bridge. It was blanketed with snow, making it look frailer as icicles feathered off every bare board. If only there were a way to obtain the funds to repair the bridge, his worries about finding a job would be taken care of.

You could ask Beth Ann for a loan.

He ignored that niggling voice in his head as he had each time it had brought up the idea. He hated the idea of begging from her, and if she offered him the money, it would negate the terms of her *aenti*'s will. The money was supposed to be used for her own happiness, not anyone else's.

Tommy's small hand grasped his. "If you want to fix the bridge, Robert, you can use my blocks."

His throat grew thick with emotion. "*Danki.* If the bridge gets fixed, I'll ask you to help. Okay?"

The little boy puffed out his narrow chest. "Okay, and I'll show you how to use them."

"*Gut.*"

Robert watched the *kind* rush forward to catch up with Beth Ann and his siblings. Sweet happiness pumped through his veins. She'd been right when she told him the youngsters would warm up to him if he was himself around them. Or one aspect of himself, he corrected. As long as his temper remained cooped up within him, everything should be fine.

When she chased after the kids when they ran into the fresh snow on the green, she turned and fell backward into the snow. "C'mon! Try it!"

The *kinder* copied her motion. As she rocked her arms and feet and called for them to do the same to make snow angels, he watched in disbelief. Beth Ann was acting as if she were no older than they were.

She motioned to him. "C'mon, Robert! Try it. I promise it won't hurt."

"I don't think—"

"That's right! Don't think."

He hesitated as she rolled to one side and stood without disturbing the pattern in the snow. She bent to lift Tommy and Crystal from the snow and held out a hand to Dougie. They turned to admire the results.

"Aren't you going to try it?" Crystal asked him. "We need a whole family of angels in the snow."

Family? Wouldn't it be *wunderbaar* if that was what they truly were? In the snow, with no interference from reality, they could be. Looking at where Beth Ann was chatting avidly with the boys, he had to wonder why he had waited so long.

"Look out!" he shouted before propelling himself toward a section of untouched snow. The kids yelled in excitement as he wiggled his legs and arms as if swimming on his back.

As he got to his feet, the younger *kinder* rushed forward to hug him and exclaim about his tall snow angel. His gaze met Beth Ann's, and the wondrous warmth rushed through him anew. He grinned, delighting in the special moment with her and the youngsters. It couldn't last, because the *kinder* might not be in Evergreen Corners much longer. He might not be, either, but he was going to relish this joy while he could.

Chapter Twelve

B eth Ann wasn't the only one wiping tears from her eyes a week later as Glen Landis handed Mr. O'Hearn a Bible inscribed with the names of the volunteers who'd helped raise the house. Harry O'Hearn and his wife, Juliet, had pitched in, helping to build homes for others while they'd lived with relatives in a house as cramped as her little cabin. Not once had they shown any impatience when others, whose need was greater, got a new house.

More than a year after Hurricane Kevin had flooded Evergreen Corners, they were the ones now being welcomed home. As Beth Ann looked at the house, she thought about the people who'd helped build it. Roofers had battled rain and wind and snow to get the shingles in place. Painters had despaired of getting their job done as storm followed storm. Inside, the doorknobs matched, thanks to Robert's efforts to make sure everything was as it was supposed to be.

One more house needed to be finished, and from the outside, it looked done. However, there remained more than a month's work inside. In fact, she guessed the volunteers would be scrambling to finish the last details as the February 1 deadline drew near. Many were heading home to enjoy Christmas with family and would return after the beginning of the New Year.

She wasn't sure what would happen once the final house was handed over to its owners. Robert might leave Evergreen Corners. She'd stay as long as the children were in her care. After that, she had no more idea what she'd do than when she'd arrived in the small town. That hadn't changed.

Everything else had. She'd fallen in love,

four times over, with Robert and the children. They'd become an odd sort of family who didn't live under the same roof but cared about one another. Each time she sat with the children at the table Robert had made, it felt as if their circle was complete.

It was an illusion.

Glen's voice freed her from her sad musings. "Let us close with a verse from Deuteronomy 28. The sixth verse. 'You will be blessed when you come in and blessed when you go out.'" He smiled at the O'Hearns and at the crowd gathered in front of the house. "Each time you open the door to your home, let the blessings of the Lord be with you and those you welcome."

Applause broke out, and someone started to sing the doxology, "Praise God from whom all blessings flow..." Others joined in with the chorus, which they repeated twice. As the last voice faded away, hugs were exchanged.

"A lovely ceremony," Robert said, standing between her and Isaac on what, in the spring, would become the house's front lawn.

"It never grows old," Beth Ann replied. "So often when we do *gut* for others, our efforts are small, quiet triumphs for God. Not in Evergreen Corners."

"We've been blessed by becoming a blessing for others," said Isaac.

She understood why her Amish friends hoped the lot would fall upon Isaac Kauffman as their first ordained minister. His faith was as much a part of him as his heartbeat, and he rejoiced in each example of God's grace in his life.

Rachel and Abby came to stand with her as the men went to answer a question Glen asked them on behalf of the new homeowners. Rachel was dabbing a tissue at her eyes, which were filled with happy tears.

"Today," Abby said, "makes the hard work worth it."

"Everyone will forget the scraped knuckles and aching muscles and the days when nothing went right." Rachel chuckled. "Giving birth to a house might be like giving birth to a *kind*. The struggle is forgotten when joy arrives."

Beth Ann smiled. "Falling in love with their babies happens quickly."

"Too bad it isn't as easy to know when the right man comes alone, ain't so?" asked Rachel. "It took me long enough to see what was right in front of my eyes. I never guessed when I came here I'd meet someone like Isaac." She glanced at the man everyone knew would be her future husband. "He has plans for the years ahead of us. Not just for our family, but for everyone in our growing community."

"Enough to keep us busy!" Abby laughed. "I need to get back to make sure everything's on track for tonight's meal."

"I need to go, too." Beth Ann thought about telling Robert she was leaving, but he was deep in conversation with Isaac and Glen.

"Where are you off to, Beth Ann?" Rachel asked. "I thought Abby was the busiest woman in Evergreen Corners, but—"

"You both make *me* tired watching all you do," Abby interrupted with a laugh. "Don't forget, Beth Ann, that you've got a whole community to help you with the Henderson *kinder*."

"Everyone has already been so helpful," she said. "The clothing for the children and the bags of groceries on the stairs have been wonderful. I don't know how you sneak them up the stairs without us noticing."

The two women exchanged a puzzled glance.

Abby said, "We haven't sent groceries to you. Meals, *ja*, but not groceries."

Beth Ann looked at Rachel, who shook her head. "I can't take credit for something I didn't do."

"So if you didn't send groceries for us, who did?"

"Maybe," Rachel said, "Pastor Hershey and his congregation or one of the other churches in town."

"I've already asked him. Back when the first deliveries came. He told me it wasn't the Mennonite congregation. It might be one of the other churches, but which one? There hasn't been a single note in any of the bags, but it has to be someone who knows the children because the bags contain their favorite foods."

"Beth Ann, you don't have to have an answer for everything," Rachel said. "Sometimes, we just need to say a prayer to thank our unknown benefactors."

Realizing Robert's sister was correct, Beth Ann nodded. She must accept the blessings and stop questioning them. Yet, curiosity teased her.

She told her friends she'd see them later. She needed to do a couple of loads of laundry and figure out what to serve for supper. The pantry shelves were quite full, though no new groceries had been left since before Thanksgiving. Adding going to the grocery store to her long chores list was going to be necessary by week's end.

"Leaving already?" asked Robert as he caught up with her by the green.

She hadn't realized he was following her. "I want to get things done before the children get home."

"How's it going with Dougie and Crystal at the Millers' house?"

"They seem to like studying with Kevin and Rosina, because they're close to the same age. I thought about having Tommy join them, but he loves his new friends at the church."

"Michael said they've fit right in with his kids, and they're polite and respectful and working hard." He raised his brows. "I never thought I'd hear anyone describe Dougie as either polite or respectful."

"He's doing better with me, too."

"He seems to like challenging me at every turn."

She looked up at him as they crossed the green. "Robert, you've usurped him as head of his family. He was the man of the house, making sure his brother and sister were fed and safe, until we came along. You and I are making the decisions, and his nose is out of joint."

"I never thought about that."

"Children are like sponges. They soak up everything around themselves. As they grow, they've got to learn what aspects of things they've experienced they want to keep."

"So as adults, we're supposed to have the perspective to know what's *gut* for us and what isn't?"

"That's how it should work." She smiled. "It's bizarre when I hear my grandmother's words coming out of my mouth while I'm dealing with the kids. What a laugh she would get out of hearing me saying things like 'Stop making such a face before it freezes that way.'"

When he twisted his face into a comical expression, she laughed. He joined in as he led the way up the apartment steps.

She reached for the keys in her purse, and he grew serious as he patted the pockets in his coat and his trousers.

"What's wrong, Robert?"

"I think I've misplaced my keys." He checked his right trouser pocket again.

"When did you last see them?"

He shrugged. "I was up early to shovel your stairs, and—"

"Robert!" The mayor stood at the bottom of the stairs. "Are you missing your keys?"

He descended, Beth Ann following close on his heels.

"Ja," he said. "Where did you find them?"

"On the ground by my porch steps."

"They must have fallen out of my pocket when I was shoveling your sidewalk." He took them. *"Danki."*

"Thank *you* for clearing the walk." She smiled at them. "I want you to know I may have found funding to at least start the covered bridge's repair. No guarantees, but I'm looking into it."

His broad smile was all the answer he needed to give.

As the two discussed possible funding, Beth Ann listened and prayed God would keep Robert in Evergreen Corners.

Robert stood to one side of the party at the community center. Many of the plain volunteers had finished eating. Some would leave in the morning to start their journeys home. For the ones who'd come the farthest, the trip could take three days or more. Those who lived in Evergreen Corners lingered over *kaffi* and dessert.

He heard whispers beneath the conversation. Michael had told him earlier that there'd been another theft at the remaining project house. A whole box of tools, not a large box, but one holding valuable power tools, was missing. A slider to the dining room had been forced open, and it was assumed someone reached in and grabbed the first thing they could put their hands on.

Nobody wanted to be talking about a thief in the days leading up to Christmas, but the authorities had been alerted. The local and county police agreed to drive past the project house, but Robert doubted they'd catch the thief, who'd been cautious so far.

When a surge of cold air announced the door opening, he looked across the room to see Beth Ann had arrived with the Henderson *kinder*. Dougie and Crystal had been at youth choir practice at the same church where Tommy went to day care. He took a single step toward them, but paused as Tommy tossed aside his coat before running to him, his gait more even with his new lime-green brace that peeked out above his boots.

"See? I got penders!" The little boy hooked his thumbs under his black suspenders and pulled them before letting them snap. "Like you, Robert."

"Suspenders," corrected his sister. "They're called suspenders."

Tommy refused to have his excitement muted. "Whatever they're called, I've got them, too." Without a pause, he turned to a table of volunteers and announced, "Look! I got penders! I mean, *sub*-penders."

As the little boy was congratulated, Robert watched Beth Ann walk toward him. His heart raced and his breath slowed until he wasn't sure he was pulling in air. She was so beautiful, so caring, and she seemed to have found her place in the world. At least for now. Was there anywhere for him in it?

He knew the answer. No, there wasn't.

Trying to keep his pain from showing on his face, he smiled when Beth Ann stopped beside him. "Those are quite the suspenders."

"I found them at Mrs. Weiskopf's store on a dusty shelf." She grinned at the little boy, who seemed determined to show off his suspenders to each person in the community center. "Did you know she's thinking of selling the store?"

"No," he said at the same time someone else asked, "Really?"

Beth Ann nodded as Dougie joined them after circling the room to see who was there. "She's mentioned to me the last two times I was in there she's thinking of moving to Florida to live with her sister."

Abby stuck her head around the kitchen door. "She's been saying that since I got here a year ago."

Going to Abby, Crystal asked, "When do we eat? I'm hungry."

"Me, too." Tommy, as always, refused to be left out of any conversation.

"Our turn is coming," Beth Ann said with

a smile. "The kitchen has had to feed a lot of people tonight."

Robert nodded. "As soon as a table is cleared, it'll be your turn." Squatting so he could look the kids in the eyes, he said, "I'd guess Abby might be willing to make you a church spread sandwich while you wait."

"Church spread?" Dougie regarded him with skepticism. "What's that?"

"Peanut butter and marshmallow."

"Let's ask Abby," Tommy said, tugging on his brother's sleeve.

"Yes," Crystal seconded. "Maybe we can help."

Robert watched as they scurried into the kitchen, calling to Abby. "You're going to owe Abby a big favor."

"I owe everyone in town for so many blessings I've lost count," Beth Ann replied. "I've been told trying to count those blessings is something I shouldn't do. I should be grateful for others' kindness and God's grace."

"Shouldn't we all?"

When he saw how her eyes glowed with

happiness, he sent up a grateful prayer of his own along with a plea God would find him a way to stay in Evergreen Corners with Beth Ann. Was it possible? He had no idea, but he was going to try his best.

The youth choir concert was set for Friday, one week before Christmas Eve on a windy, cold evening. In the past, the choir had performed in the high school's gym, but the space hadn't been rebuilt yet, so the program was being held in what everyone called the "little gym" of the elementary school. It was a smaller space used by kindergartners and first graders when the weather was too inclement for them to go outside after lunch. Unlike the high school's gym, it had concrete floors and a bank of windows along the outer wall. Two sets of double doors opened from the hallway and at the opposite end, two other doors led outside. A simple wooden seat ran beneath the windows from one exterior door to the other.

At both ends, basketball hoops had been

pulled up to the ceiling from their normal spot six feet above the floor, the low height making it simpler for the youngest students to sink balls into the baskets. Wooden folding chairs had been arranged in neat rows. An upright piano sat to the left of two rows of risers, and a music stand waited in front.

Beth Ann walked with Tommy into the little gym. The wall behind the risers had been covered with long sheets of paper decorated with what she guessed was a Nativity scene drawn in crayon. The camels resembled the cows, and the sheep looked like either dachshunds or earthbound clouds, because some had no legs. The baby in the manger was as big as the depictions of Joseph and Mary while the angel appeared to be in danger of slipping down the slanted roof of the stable. It was obvious the children had put in a lot of time, and it'd been a labor of love. She glanced down at the folded program she'd been given and saw Crystal's name among the other young artists listed.

"There he is!" Tommy announced so

loudly heads turned. He hurried to where Robert sat.

She smiled. His gait was much better. It was uneven, as her own was, but with the brace helping correct his slap step, he didn't look as if he might tip over on every other step.

Her smile broadened when Robert picked up his hat from two seats beside him. He and Tommy were already chatting about the suspenders the little boy had insisted on wearing.

Looking past the boy, Robert greeted her with a smile that sent tickles of happiness along her. He shifted so Tommy would sit on her right side, and Robert had the chair on her left.

"Thank you for coming," she murmured as the door from the hall opened and the pianist came in to polite clapping.

"I wouldn't miss watching this with you for the world," he replied.

The tickles became stronger ripples, and she was glad she was prevented from answering by the youth choir following their director into the gym. While the children climbed onto the risers and parents raised their cell phones to begin recording, Beth Ann picked out Dougie in the middle row among the boys. Crystal was on the left-hand side with the other smallest girls. Both wore the most serious expressions she'd ever seen on their faces.

The youth choir began to sing "The First Noel." When they did the next verse in harmony, she heard gasps of appreciation. The oldest child couldn't be more than twelve, and the youngest Crystal's age, and their youthful voices wove around the melody in a lush sound that filled the gym.

When they finished, there was a moment of silence. Applause burst out from appreciative family, friends and neighbors before the choir started its next song. Each number was as amazing as the first while the songs told the glorious story of the Savior's birth.

Beth Ann's eyes widened when Dougie edged past the boy in front of him and stepped forward. He looked around the crowd, and his gaze met hers. When she saw fear in his eyes, she offered a bolstering smile, though she wondered what was happening. He gave her one in return.

The music director bent and murmured something to him, too low for anyone else to hear. Dougie nodded and gulped hard, but he straightened his shoulders as she faced the choir and raised her hands. She nodded to the pianist, who began playing the introduction to "O Holy Night."

Dougie alone began to sing, and goose bumps rose on Beth Ann's arm. His voice was pure and sweet, sending notes wafting through the gym. The words of awe and glory spun out of the boy who'd been abandoned by his mother. The other children joined in the chorus. Their treble voices lilted around his and invited the wind from beyond the gym to complement the music in a deep, rumbling undertone.

A hand settled over hers on her lap, and she tore her gaze from the choir to look at Robert. Were those tears in his eyes like the ones filling her throat while they listened to the boy—*their* boy—sing beautifully? Tommy leaned his head against her and wrapped his short arms around hers.

She knew, without question, this was what she wanted. A life with a family who loved one another. Though she wasn't sure how Robert felt about her or the children, she knew each of them was in her heart.

The last note died away, and thunderous applause and cheers erupted through the gym. One person, then others rose as the music director gestured toward Dougie, who took a solemn bow before joining the other children. Beth Ann stood, too, and peered around a tall woman in front of her until she caught the boy's eyes. She raised her hands over her head, so he could see her clapping.

The choir did a rousing version of "Joy to the World" as their encore and took a bow along with their director and the pianist before breaking ranks to join their families. Beth Ann held out her arms and swept Dougie and Crystal to her.

Dougie tried to wriggle away. His face, which had glowed when he was singing, had regained its sullen expression. "Don't make a big deal of it, okay?"

Seeing her shock mirrored in Robert's eyes, Beth Ann said, "Dougie, it's okay to admit how important the choir is to you."

He shook his head. "No, it's not."

She put a hand on his shoulder before he could move away from her. "Why not?"

"You know!"

"I don't."

"You should. You loved being a midwife, but that was taken away from you. You loved your family, and that was taken away from you, too."

She sat on a chair at the end of one row and drew him down next to her. Behind him, his siblings and Robert formed a protective half circle. "So you believe if we admit how much we love something, it'll be taken away from us."

"Yeah. That's the way life is."

Wishing she could reach inside him and tear out the cancerous cynicism, she said, "No, it's not."

"It is!" He stamped his foot. "Everything

I've ever loved has gone away. My dad, my mom...everything."

She cupped his face in her hands and waited in silence until his eyes met hers. Not letting him look away, she whispered, "I'm sorry, Dougie, about what you've lost, but you've got Crystal and Tommy. You've got me. You've got Robert. You've got the Millers and others who care for you."

"I wish my mom could have heard me tonight." His lips trembled.

"I wish she could have, too." She gave him a sudden smile. "I saw other parents were filming the concert. I'm sure one of them would be glad to share a copy so you can show it to your mother."

"When? We can't see her in rehab."

"I don't know when, but why don't you ask one of your friends in the choir for a copy you can show her as soon as possible?"

Crystal piped up, "I'll do that, Dougie." She went to speak to a woman who was congratulating her daughter on the successful concert.

The woman listened to Crystal, straightened and smiled. She wrote something on a piece of paper and handed it to Crystal, who brought it to Beth Ann. It was the woman's name and her phone number.

"Thank you," Beth Ann said. "Merry Christmas."

The woman nodded before leaving with her husband and four children.

Turning to Dougie, Beth Ann said, "See? Your mother is going to have a chance to hear you sing and see Crystal's beautiful work." She gripped the boy by the elbows. "As soon as possible, we'll make sure she sees it."

Robert put his hand on Dougie's shoulder. "It's not the Amish way to say we're proud of someone, but there's nothing in our *Ordnung* that says we can't go to the diner for a burger and fries to celebrate the next-to-last week of Advent."

The *kinder* cheered at his words.

"This is the best day ever," Crystal said as she flung her arms around his waist. "Right, Dougie?"

"It's not bad," her brother agreed.

When everyone else laughed, he joined in. Beth Ann stood, glad the storm had passed again. She planned to call their social worker on Monday and find out when it would be possible for the children to visit their mother. It might be the best Christmas gift she could give them.

If it was possible.

Chapter Thirteen

The following Monday, Beth Ann dried the last bowl and put it in the cupboard, closing the door. She reached for the dishrag to wipe down the top of the stove. Making chili tonight for the children had been an inspired idea. The recipe Abby had shared with her had been simple and straightforward. The results had been a success, and the kitchen smelled of onions and chili powder. Though she'd eaten her fill, the scent was tantalizing.

"You missed it!" she heard Dougie say from the living room. "She cooked us a delicious meal."

"Is that so?" Robert asked as she walked in.

She wasn't sure if she would have recognized him if not for his voice. He wore earmuffs under his black hat, and a striped red-and-blue scarf wrapped around the neck of his sedate coat and reached halfway up his face.

She hadn't expected him to stop by tonight, though she had hoped to talk to him soon and get his advice. Earlier in the day, while she'd been at the community center to pick up lunch for the volunteers at the project house, she'd received a call from her aunt's attorney. The money would soon be released, and she needed to decide where she wanted it deposited. She'd agreed to contact the lawyer tomorrow or the next day with her answer.

But she had no idea what it would be.

As she'd hung up, she'd noticed several people looking at her. Had she talked too loudly? Other than Robert, she hadn't told anyone about the inheritance. She'd grabbed the box with the meals and headed to the project house. There, she hadn't had a chance during work to tell Robert about the call, and she didn't want to talk about it in front of the children now.

Hooking a finger in the top of his scarf, Robert drew it down enough to ask, "How about a driving lesson?"

"Now? It's eight o'clock, and if the puff of air that came in with you is any sign, it's cold outside."

"It's not bad if you're bundled up, and Gladys said she'd be glad to babysit." He didn't add more before a knock came at the door.

"You asked her before you asked me?"

"Let's not leave the mayor out in the cold." He opened the door and smiled when Gladys scurried in, as bundled up as he was.

The mayor smiled. "I hope you two plan on doing something indoors. It's far too cold for December!"

"I was going to give Beth Ann a driving lesson," he said. "There's a battery-operated heater in the buggy. We should be okay."

Both of them as well as the children focused on Beth Ann. Though she didn't want to brave the cold, the idea of being alone with Robert—with no children as chaperones—was at the top of her list.

"I guess a few minutes won't hurt," she said, but couldn't keep from smiling.

Dougie made a disgusted sound; Robert grinned. He wanted to spend time alone with her, too. If he was willing to challenge the cold, she was as well.

Getting her coat and her bonnet and two scarves and another of the mayor's, she pulled those on before she took her gloves out of her pockets. She told the children to behave for Gladys and reminded them there were cookies for a treat.

The cold swept her breath away as Beth Ann stepped onto the landing. Hurrying down the steps in Robert's wake, she climbed into the buggy without greeting Clipper, who was stamping his feet to stay warm.

"We shouldn't keep him out long," she said when Robert was sitting beside her. "He doesn't have a heat box."

"I figured a couple of times around the green would be sufficient tonight." He smiled in the dim light hanging above the dashboard. "There's not a lot of traffic, so it's a *gut* time for you to practice." He handed her the reins. "Do you remember how to hold these?"

Concentrating on arranging the reins through her fingers, which were clumsy in the thick gloves, she stiffened for a moment when he shifted closer to her and his arms encircled her. He put his hands on the reins next to hers. Surrounded by his strength, she had to fight her own yearning to lean back on his broad chest.

"All right," he said, his breath sifting through his scarf and hers, "give him the command to start."

She struggled to focus on her task when every motion of the buggy down the steep road bounced her against him. Listening to his instructions, she steered the buggy around the corner and toward the store.

"Look at that!" she exclaimed, pointing with her elbow to a for-sale sign tacked to the general store's porch. "Mrs. Weiskopf is serious about leaving town. I wonder what it would be like to run a store where everyone in town comes in and shops. Wouldn't it be fun to be able to help people like that?"

"I'd rather spend time creating something beautiful, whether it's a bookcase or a table."

She gazed at the store. "I think I'd love having a place like that. Working regular hours and being able to help people instead of being called out to deliver babies. I—"

"Beth Ann, pay attention to the road," Robert ordered as the high beams from an approaching truck flashed in the rearview mirrors.

She maneuvered the buggy closer to the curb, and the truck zoomed around them, going too fast for the village streets.

As they turned to go along the other side of the green, Robert moved away from her and let her take control of the buggy. She missed the warmth of him, but she had to think about steering the buggy and keeping Clipper at a steady pace.

"Robert, I wanted to talk to you about something important," she said when the buggy began to slow as it went up the hill.

"More important than driving the buggy?"

"I can drive and talk at the same time. I think."

"You won't know unless you try."

After outlining what the attorney had told her, she asked, "What do you think I should do with the money?"

"Your *aenti* wanted you to spend it on something to make you happy."

"I'm happy now." She *was* happy being with Robert and the children in Evergreen Corners. The future was still a puzzle she hadn't solved, but she was happy.

"Now?" he asked, his voice dropping into a husky rasp.

The sound sent shivers along her that had nothing to do with the cold. "Yes," she whispered.

He drew the reins out of her hands and steered the buggy toward the curb, bringing the horse to a halt. "I am, too, Beth Ann."

"Thank you for all you're doing for me and the children."

"I wish it could be more."

"You've done more than I had any right to expect when I dragged you into this situation." She leaned in to kiss his cheek.

His hands reached out to grasp her elbows, stopping her. Embarrassment seared her, but vanished as his fingers slipped up to her shoulders as his arms enveloped her. He pulled her to him, and her lips were met by his. The warmth she had seen earlier in his eyes caressed her mouth. Giving herself to the perfection of his embrace, she curved her arms up his back.

When he drew his mouth from hers, he whispered, "Open your eyes."

She ignored his words, wanting to linger in this wondrous dream of being in his arms with his mouth against hers.

"Beth Ann, please," he murmured.

She looked up at him as she ran a bold fingertip along his firm jaw. Turning his head, he teased her gloved fingers with a light kiss. He murmured her name as he bent to capture her lips again.

Clipper stamped his feet, rocking the buggy.

Robert released her. "I think he's ready to get back to his warm stall." He reached for the reins, but paused and kissed her again.

As he drove them toward the apartment, she shifted on the seat so she could lean her head on his shoulder. Once she left the buggy, reality would hit and she'd have to face the truth about how impossible it was for them to share more than these few stolen kisses. Nothing had changed. He was Amish. She wasn't.

What if you were? The question bounced through her head, followed by more. If she were Amish, could she be licensed as a foster parent and keep the Henderson kids under her roof? She didn't know any Amish people who fostered children. Some took in family members or neighbors' children for days or even years, but being licensed by the state might not be allowed.

She didn't want to choose between Robert and the children. She wanted all of them in her life, but the truth was, within weeks, each one of them could be gone.

Beth Ann stiffened when she heard someone shout Robert's name. He turned the buggy toward the curb again, and she realized they were in front of the community center.

Michael Miller ran up to the door. "Robert, I've been looking for you. Oh, Beth Ann!"

"I've been teaching her to drive the buggy," Robert said as if it were the most unexpected thing in the world.

"I need to speak with you." His face was taut as he looked from Robert to her. "Both of you."

"What's wrong?" she asked.

"Can we talk inside?" Michael wrapped his arms around himself and stamped his feet as Clipper had.

Beth Ann almost shouted to Robert to whip up the horse and get them away from whatever bad news Michael had, but she said, "All right."

* * *

Pausing to throw a blanket over Clipper, smoothing it across the horse's back, Robert followed Michael and Beth Ann into the community center. Why had Michael intruded? Robert had something to tell her, too, something that might ruin everything he'd hoped for. No, it *would* ruin everything, which was why he'd kissed her while he could. He wouldn't have the chance again after she learned he'd been offered a job at the hardware store in Rutland. The pay was excellent, and the hours *gut*, leaving him time to spend on his woodworking. It was everything he'd prayed for.

Except it was too far away from her and the *kinder*. Worse, once the kids were placed elsewhere, she'd be alone in Evergreen Corners and she might decide to leave. With the money from her *aenti*'s bequest, she could go anywhere.

Now wasn't the time to tell her, not when Michael could hear at the same time. A part of him was relieved, but he must tell her soon.

When Michael led them to the hall between the community center and the chapel, the cold hallway was lit only by exit signs. He flipped a switch, and a single lamp came on about halfway along it. Set on a table holding hymn books, the lamp offered enough light so Robert could see the strain on his friend's face.

"What's up?" He was pleased he was able to put a positive spin on the question. Maybe if he stayed optimistic, the discussion would end up okay. He was fooling himself. A single glance at the tension tightening his friend's mouth was warning enough that something was wrong. Very wrong.

Michael glanced around again, as if he expected eavesdroppers loitering in the shadows, before he asked, his breath hanging in the air, "Will you understand if we speak in *Deitsch*, Beth Ann?"

"I know enough to get along in most conversations. If I can't get what you're saying, I'll ask."

With a nod, he switched to the language

the Amish used among themselves. "*Gut.* I'd rather not have to worry about any *Englisch* folks hearing us." Looking at Robert, he said, "Kevin's mentioned to me today that Douglas has new toys Kevin thinks are 'cool.' His word, not mine."

"New toys?" repeated Beth Ann. As Michael began to explain, she waved his words aside. "I got what you said, but the *kinder* don't have any new toys."

"Kevin said Douglas was showing off a handheld computer game. Douglas hid it in his backpack when Cora came to check on their desk work."

She glanced at Robert. "Did you buy the *kinder* presents for Christmas?"

"I did," he replied, "but not a handheld computer game."

"So where did Douglas get it?" asked Michael, bringing Robert's attention to him.

"I don't know." He looked at Beth Ann.

She shook her head. "I don't know, either."

Michael drew in a deep breath. "I don't want to accuse the boy, but I keep thinking about the thefts at the work sites."

Robert nodded. "Those have been going on for months, ain't so?"

"We had a few in the fall, and they stopped." Michael met his gaze steadily. "They started again a couple weeks of ago, which is why we began locking the tools away."

Beth Ann's brows lowered. "Who has a key?"

"Each of our team leaders does," Robert said. "Four of us. Michael, Jose Lopez, Vernon Umble and me. Except for me, the others have been working on and off for more than a year."

"Is the key on your key ring?"

Dismay dropped through him like a rock over a cliff. *"Ja."* He told Michael about losing his keys while shoveling snow. "They were out of my possession for no more than an hour or two."

Michael waved aside his words. "That was only a few days ago. These robberies have been going on for at least two weeks, and…"

"Dougie had the game today," Beth Ann

said. "I hope the two aren't connected, Michael, but I'll talk to Dougie when we get home."

"*We* will," added Robert. "It's time to get answers about a lot of things."

Though Beth Ann hoped the conversation with Dougie would go well, it turned sour from the moment the younger children were put to bed and she and Robert asked Dougie to join them in the kitchen. Dougie slouched in his chair and wouldn't look in their direction as Robert outlined what they'd been told.

"Kevin has a big mouth for such a little kid." Dougie clamped his arms to his chest and glowered. "He doesn't know what he's talking about."

"No?" asked Robert. "What reason would Kevin have to lie about you showing off a fancy new computer toy?"

"I dunno."

"Where's the toy?" Beth Ann asked.

"I don't have it."

"Do you know where it is?" Robert's tone

harshened. "Playing word games might be fun on that computer, Dougie, but it's not going to work with us."

"I told you. I don't have it, and I don't know where it is."

"Where was it when you last saw it?"

The boy shrugged.

Beth Ann put a hand on Robert's arm. His tension was palpable through his sleeve. "Robert..."

He ignored her as he locked eyes with the boy. "Are you going to add lying to your sin of stealing?"

"I didn't steal anything." The boy jumped up and stood on tiptoe in an effort to put his face close to Robert's. "Don't call me a thief!"

"I won't call you a thief if you confess how you got the money for that toy!"

"None of your business!"

Robert clenched his fingers into fists and took a single step toward the boy.

Beth Ann had heard and seen enough. "Stop this, both of you! Dougie, we'll talk in the morning. Go to bed."

"It's too early—"

"Go to bed. If you can't sleep, take the time to think about what you've done and said and ask God's forgiveness."

"What about him?" He hooked a thumb at Robert, who had moved away to lean one hand on the counter.

"I'm going to give him the same advice."

When Dougie opened his mouth to retort, she scowled and pointed to the living room. The boy swaggered out of the kitchen as if he'd won the argument.

She ignored his attitude and looked at Robert as she closed the door to the other room. He appeared more distressed than he'd been when Michael sought them out at the community center.

"Give him time, Robert," she said.

"To do what? Create more trouble?" He winced and lowered his eyes.

She wasn't sure what in his few words had sent pain through him. "Yelling at him won't make him honest. He's as stubborn as you are."

"So how do you suggest we convince him to be honest with us?"

"Dougie has to be willing to trust us."

"That's not an answer. That's..." Again he grimaced.

"What is it?" she asked.

He shook his head. "Nothing. Tired of quarreling." Pushing away from the counter, he said, "I need to go."

"Robert—"

"Gut nacht," he said before he walked out, slamming the kitchen door behind him.

She stared at the vibrating door, shocked at what she'd witnessed. She'd never heard Robert use a low, menacing voice as he had when speaking to Dougie. It had unsettled him, too, because he'd stopped himself twice from saying more or grabbing the boy. Had he intended to shake some sense into Dougie?

She couldn't guess. She knew only one thing with all her heart. Robert had said good-night as he stormed out of the kitchen, but deep inside her it felt like goodbye.

Chapter Fourteen

Beth Ann was startled when she opened the kitchen door after Robert's departure and saw him standing in front of her. Crystal faced him, a guilty expression in her eyes. Tears bubbled out of the little girl's eyes and rained down her cheeks.

"I should have remembered," Robert said, looking at Beth Ann with an apologetic glance, "it's impossible to guess who's listening if the door is closed."

Apologizing for not remembering or for what happened in the kitchen? She scanned the room, but didn't see Dougie. Where was the boy? She'd look for him, but first...

Pushing past Robert, she drew Crystal

into the kitchen and sat her on the chair where her brother had been moments ago. "Are you okay, sweetheart?"

"I heard shouting." Crystal's lashes glistened with tears. "I don't like shouting."

"Nobody does." Beth Ann cut her eyes to Robert, who hadn't left the apartment as she'd feared he would.

"Dougie shut himself in the bathroom," the little girl said, clasping her hands tightly in her lap.

"Thank you for telling me," Beth Ann said gently.

"I've got something else to tell you." She dropped her voice to a near whisper. "Dougie doesn't think I know, but I do."

"What do you know?" Beth Ann asked.

"About the money he used to buy toys and how he got it."

Firing a glance at Robert because she didn't want him to get angry at the girl as he had with Dougie, she asked, "Will you tell us?"

Crystal chewed on her lower lip as she considered her answer.

Beth Ann tried to keep from prodding the girl to answer. She'd never guessed waiting on a stubborn baby to make an appearance would be simple in comparison to dealing with school-aged children.

"Mommy's money," Crystal finally answered. "Her 'just-in-case' money."

"Just in case of what?"

Crystal's eyes widened. "I don't know. She never said."

Beth Ann could think of several reasons Kim Henderson would have stashed money away. To pay her drug dealer or to arrange for bail if arrested. Beth Ann wanted to believe maybe she'd set aside the money so her children could eat when she wasn't around, but the youngsters' conditions disproved that.

"So you all knew about the money?" Robert asked.

"Aunt Sharon didn't, and Tommy doesn't." She rolled her eyes. "Dougie says Tommy can't keep a secret so we'd be foolish to let him in on it. He said I was big enough to keep my mouth shut." She reached into her pocket and pulled out a twenty-dollar bill. "I've remembered to take out my money when putting my clothes in the laundry. Not like Dougie." She laughed. "Boy, was he mad at himself!"

The girl clamped both hands over her mouth as her eyes grew wide.

Beth Ann touched the child's arm. "It's okay, Crystal. I'm glad you're being honest. I didn't think the money belonged to Mayor Whittaker."

"You gave it to her," she said from behind her hands.

"I was waiting for you and your brothers to tell me the truth."

Crystal moaned. "Dougie is gonna kill me."

"No, he's not." Beth Ann struggled not to smile, because she knew the girl's words were heartfelt. "Where did you get the money?"

She shut her mouth as her brother had.

Beth Ann tried another tack. "Why did Dougie buy the computer toy?"

"He wanted to stop the other boys from saying bad things about us."

"What sort of bad things?" She waved her hand to halt the girl's answer. "What they say doesn't matter."

"It does to Dougie. He doesn't like being called a loser or a mooch."

Robert shook his head and sighed. "He thought if he had the latest new toy everyone wanted, he'd show them he wasn't what they said he was."

Crystal nodded, her lip quivering.

Embracing the girl, Beth Ann wished she could find a way to protect her from the unkind words. She couldn't, but she knew someone who could help.

"Let's pray God will open the hearts of those who insult your brother—"

"And me?"

"And you." She kissed the top of the child's soft red hair. "God, please open hearts to the truth about Dougie and Crystal—"

"And Tommy!"

Beth Ann was shocked. "Has someone been teasing him?"

"No, but it doesn't hurt to be careful, does it?"

With another hug, Beth Ann said, "God, please open hearts to the truth about Dougie and Crystal and Tommy, and let others see them as we see them. As Your beloved children. God, please let Dougie and Crystal and Tommy never forget You're with them and they can turn to You with their hurts."

"Amen," Robert added.

The sound of the outer door closing silenced them. Beth Ann ran into the living room. It was empty. The door to the bathroom was wide-open.

"Dougie's gone," she said.

"I'll bring him back." Robert reached for his coat.

"Robert..." She wasn't sure how to say what she must when Crystal—and Tommy, who was peeking around the bedroom door—were listening.

Facing her, Robert said, "I'll do my best

not to lose my temper again. I give you my word, Beth Ann."

She wrapped her arms around the younger children as he threw open the door and vanished into the cold night.

Crystal whispered, "Should we pray for Dougie?"

"Yes." She drew the children to her as they bowed their heads, but didn't speak the prayer coming from her heart as she prayed for both Dougie and Robert.

The boy was heading to the dilapidated house where he'd lived, Robert knew. It was dangerous for Dougie to go inside, but it wouldn't be the first time since he and Beth Ann had moved the kids in with her if Dougie had taken his *mamm*'s money.

He increased the length of his stride. He didn't want to slip on the sidewalks where spots of black ice were waiting for the unwary pedestrian, but he also had to keep the boy from going inside that condemned house, too.

Robert breathed a sigh of relief when he

saw Dougie's smaller silhouette on the corner of the Hendersons' street. Now to convince the boy to heed him...

I'll do my best not to lose my temper again. I give you my word, Beth Ann.

Shame struck him like a closed fist. Was this the final punishment his *daed* could inflict on him? A legacy of violence and rage?

No, he was forewarned, and he must lean on God's strength to help him overcome the cycle of anger. God and Beth Ann, who'd stepped in tonight and broken through frustration's red curtain to calm the beast within him.

Dougie looked back as Robert approached. For the length of a single breath, the boy poised to run, then halted, hanging his head.

Robert had never guessed he'd miss the boy's overconfidence, but he hated seeing Dougie so defeated.

"Crystal told you, ain't so?" Dougie asked when Robert stopped beside him on the windswept sidewalk.

Robert managed to hide his astonishment when Dougie used the Amish phrase. Beth Ann had warned him *kinder* were sponges.

"Your sister is worried about you," he said.

"If she was worried, she would've kept her mouth shut." He shoved his hands in his coat pockets, and Robert realized he didn't have mittens on. Or a hat or a scarf.

Taking off his scarf, he handed it to the boy. "Crystal doesn't see it that way, and neither does Beth Ann. They're scared you'll get hurt if you go into your house."

"I've been okay before."

"You're a smart kid, Dougie. The house is about to fall in. You don't want to be inside when it does, do you?"

"No." The answer was reluctant.

"Look. Let's talk to Gladys tomorrow and see what we can do about getting the house down safely."

"My mom's money—"

"We'll make sure whatever you and Crystal and Tommy want is out before the house is demolished." He held his hand out to the boy. "Okay?"

Dougie shook it. "Okay."

"Let's go back to the apartment."

Not moving, the boy asked, "You're not going to yell again?"

"No, but Beth Ann is going to want you to hand over the toy and whatever else you've bought with your *mamm*'s money."

"But—"

"Dougie, trust her and me."

"I trust Lady Bee."

Robert tried not to flinch at the insult the boy aimed at him. He couldn't fault Dougie after Robert had blown up at him in the kitchen. *"Gut,"* he said. "Trust her, because you know she cares a lot about the three of you. Let's go before we freeze."

"Do you trust me?" Dougie asked as he fell into step with Robert up the sloping sidewalk.

"You've given me your word you'll let us get your things out of that house. I'm going to trust you unless you give me a reason not to."

The boy didn't reply, but Robert couldn't miss how he walked a little taller. Again Beth Ann's voice filled his head.

Dougie has to be willing to trust us.

Robert understood she meant they needed to trust the boy, too. He hoped he could, but the thefts hung over everyone's heads. If Dougie was involved with those...

He pushed that thought from his head as he turned with the boy toward the apartment. One step at a time, and he had to believe God would lead him to the answers about the thefts, about the children, about Beth Ann and about what he should do with the job offer in Rutland. He hoped it'd be soon.

Christmas was two days away. Most of the volunteers had gone home for the holidays. For the first time, Beth Ann saw Evergreen Corners as it had been before the flood and would be after Amish Helping Hands and the other agencies closed up shop. The tattered remains of the covered bridge remained the sole blight on the village, but Gladys had reassured both her and Robert yesterday she was still chasing down possible funding. It was ironic Beth Ann soon would have more money than she'd ever imagined. Yet it wouldn't be enough to rebuild the covered bridge. That would require in the millions of dollars.

She knew she was redirecting her thoughts from Robert and the children. Dougie had given her the computer toy and another electronic device, and she'd accepted them without comment. He'd been subdued, so she'd no clue what he was thinking.

Robert acted as if the luscious kisses in the buggy had never happened, and he hid his thoughts from her.

Tommy was bouncing off the wall in anticipation of their gift exchange on Christmas morning. So far, he'd revealed he couldn't say what he planned to give her, but it had a cotton tail and antlers and was purple and he'd made it himself without much help from Gwen.

Only Crystal seemed unchanged. She

acted oblivious to what was happening around her, having discovered *A Little Princess*. Beth Ann wondered if the tale of a child who lost both her parents and was consigned to living with strangers was the best thing for Crystal to read when her own life was in an upheaval, but said nothing. If the story gave Crystal comfort and entertainment, Beth Ann was grateful.

Though everyone seemed determined to act as if everything was as it should be, she couldn't pretend she didn't hear the mumbles underlying the Christmas preparations. The thefts had people worried about the safety of their families and homes. She heard speculation about the thief's identity. The guilty looks in her direction told her what the whispers hadn't.

Dougie was suspected of being the thief because he'd been seen with the new toys. She did hear a few whispers about how she might have bought the items for the boy, because she was coming into a lot of money. The amount she chanced to overhear was more than ten times what her aunt had bequeathed to her. She guessed someone had listened to her phone call at the community center, and gossip had swept through the town faster than the floodwaters had after Hurricane Kevin.

She despaired that the only way to clear Dougie's name was to find the actual thief. She had an idea, but needed Robert's help. Hoping he'd agree, she went to the last project house where he was working on the roof. If he wouldn't help her, she'd try to make the plan work anyhow. She didn't want Deana returning on Christmas Eve and learning about the accusations aimed at Dougie. The social worker might yank the kids out of the house, and that would destroy any hope of Beth Ann giving them a happy Christmas.

As darkness and cold settled with thickly falling snow on the village in the darkest hours after midnight on Christmas Eve, Robert crouched in one corner of the mayor's garage. Beth Ann's plan had been simple. Leave the door unlocked and valuable tools in plain sight. At the project house and on the way through the village, he'd talked to everyone he met about storing the tools overnight. He hadn't shouted the words, not wanting to be too obvious, but he hadn't kept his voice down, either.

He wondered if his knees, aching with cold and hours of squatting, would straighten enough to propel him toward the door if someone took the bait. He'd had time while they waited in the cold to tell Beth Ann about his job offer, but he hadn't. He'd told himself over and over she was already too upset about the upcoming visit from the social worker. His news could wait.

Couldn't it?

He prayed they'd be able to nab the thief before Deana arrived and heard the rumors in the village. Beth Ann's scheme to prove Dougie wasn't the thief had seemed like a *gut* one in the middle of the day. He wondered if they'd been fooling themselves.

Then came the sound of furtive footfalls. He thanked God they weren't coming down the stairs from the apartment where the *kinder* were warm in their beds. No, the person was walking from the street.

Beth Ann leaned toward him and whispered, "Someone's coming."

He put his finger to her lips, but jerked it back as sweet, warm tingles climbed his arm and into his heart. He couldn't allow himself to be distracted. Not when he had no idea how the thief—if the person pushing the door wider was the thief—would react to being caught in their trap.

Beside him, she shifted, and he guessed she was trying to see who was entering the garage. Whoever stood in the doorway was backlit by the lights from the streetlamps, light sifted by the snowflakes that merged with the silhouette into a strange pattern. A coat, hat and scarf further disguised the person's shape and height.

There was no disguising the person's intent. A hand reached out and grabbed the toolbox he'd left close to the door.

He jumped to his feet and threw his arms around the thief. Shocked by how slight the person was, sickness flowed through him. Was Dougie really the thief?

The person struggled, and the ski cap flew off, revealing long hair that slapped him like a hundred separate hands. The thief threw both of them against the wall, the concussion slamming through him. He refused to let go, and the thief kept fighting.

A light blazed through the garage. Beth Ann gasped from beyond the flashlight she held, and he looked at the thief. A woman! He made sure his hold was secure but wouldn't hurt her. She cursed at him with language he hadn't heard since his *daed* dropped a heavy sledgehammer on his toe.

"What's going on down here?" came a shout from the door. Dougie!

Robert tightened his arms as the woman redoubled her efforts to escape. "Run to Gladys's. Call 911!" he shouted as the woman tried to flee again.

Instead of obeying, Dougie ran into the garage. He gulped twice before asking, "Mommy? Mommy, what are you doing here?"

Beth Ann rushed forward to catch Dougie before the little boy could reach Robert and the woman. Shock widened her bright green eyes when she looked from the *kind* to the red-haired woman Dougie had called *Mamm*.

The truth hit Robert as hard as Kim Henderson had. Somehow she must have slipped away from the rehab center. She'd been stealing tools and selling them to get the drugs she craved. It was a scenario none of them had imagined.

The next few minutes became a blur as the cops were called and put handcuffs on Kim. Robert held his arm around Dougie's shoulders. Both to comfort the boy and to keep him away from his *mamm*. Sorrow rushed through him.

"Don't let them hurt Mommy!" cried Tommy from the snow-covered stairs as the police guided a thrashing Kim to their patrol car.

"They won't." Beth Ann picked up the little boy and drew Crystal to her. "They want to help her."

"How? By throwing her in jail?" cried Dougie, pulling away.

Robert caught him again. Dougie stopped trying to elude him when the patrol car door closed, the noise loud in the quiet night.

As Beth Ann guided all three *kinder* up the stairs, the patrol car pulled slowly away from the curb and out into the thick snow on the street.

Closing the garage door, Robert turned to find Gladys behind him.

She put a hand on his sleeve. "We'll take care of this. Go help Beth Ann. She's going to need you more than ever."

"Ja." He nodded his thanks and took the stairs, three at once, not caring about the snow that threatened to send him crashing to his knees on every step.

He bumped into Beth Ann when he opened the door, but she moved aside without speaking. Her face, shadowed in the dim light from the kitchen, looked as if she'd aged a lifetime since they'd captured Kim Henderson in their simple trap. He took her place by the door, and she faced three angry, terrified, confused *kinder*.

"You can't see her now," she said in a tone that suggested she'd already repeated those words several times.

"She's our mother!" Dougie's lips trembled in the same uneven tempo as his hands as he held them out in a voiceless plea. "They're going to throw her in jail! Throw her in jail and throw away the key. That's what Aunt Sharon said would happen if she got caught again."

"No!" cried Crystal and Tommy at the same time. "Not Mommy!"

Crystal ran across the room to Beth Ann. "Don't let them hurt Mommy."

"Nobody's going to hurt her," Beth Ann said. "Everyone wants to help her."

"Don't put her in jail!" insisted Dougie. "How's that going to help her?"

Robert wondered what he could say to reach the *kinder*. "Dougie, it's the best thing for your *mamm*."

"What do you know about what's best for

326 An Amish Holiday Family

her? You don't know her. You think she's a bad person."

"You're right. I don't know her, so I can't judge her. But I've seen how she abandoned you and your sister and brother in a house falling down around you."

"She can't help it! She's sick."

"She'll get the help she needs if she'll stay where there are people to help her."

"We could help her." He whirled toward Beth Ann. "You can help her, can't you, Lady Bee? You've helped us, especially Tommy. He's walking much better."

"Dougie," she began, "I don't know how—"

"That's not true! You didn't know anything about taking care of kids, but you took us." His mouth dropped into a fierce frown. "Or were you doing it for yourself? Do something good for the poor kids of a druggie, and you get everyone to think you're wonderful?"

"Enough!" she snapped in a tone he'd never heard her use.

Anger.

She was angry and wasn't trying to hide her feelings. Her eyes blazed with green fire that threatened to scorch the boy if he spoke another word.

Knowing what he risked, for his own anger was surging, he ordered, "Douglas Henderson, be quiet! You need to listen to Beth Ann. She—"

"Enough from you, too, Robert!" She continued to scowl at Dougie, but her voice softened. "Where did you get the idea I agreed to take care of you because I wanted people to think I was wonderful?"

"That's what Aiden Bryson said," the boy said.

It took Robert a moment to place the name. It belonged to the boy Dougie had hit at school. "What?"

"That's what he said before I knocked him on his butt."

"I had no idea," she whispered. "I thought he said something about you and Crystal."

"He did! Me and Crystal, we know we're not what people say. You're a good person, Lady Bee, and he shouldn't have said nasty things about you." He gulped. "I'm sorry I just did that, too."

"Don't ever be sorry that you've told me how you feel. Not ever." She pulled him to her and put her arms around him as he buried his face against her coat. He began to sob, as if every ache in his heart was released. When the other children moved closer, she widened her arms to bring them into her embrace.

Robert never had felt so alone as when he stood outside the circle of love in front of him. Not even in his darkest hours after Rachel had run away and he'd wondered if God had deserted him, too, as their *daed*'s rage focused on him. He didn't step forward, despite knowing she'd welcome him as she did the *kinder*.

He hung his head. He didn't deserve to be part of their affirmation of love. Not after nearly losing his temper...again.

A knock at the door behind him startled him. Beth Ann looked up, her face lined with worry.

Robert opened the door. A policeman

stood on the other side, his uniform almost concealed in snow. It was falling even harder and blowing on erratic gusts of wind.

"Does Beth Ann Overholt live here?"

As she nodded and went to the door, the *kinder* looked at one another in horror. Robert wanted to reassure them the officer wasn't here to take her away, too. But why was the cop at her door? The capture of Kim Henderson should have cleared Dougie from any suspicion.

"Can I come in?" asked the policeman, who gave his name as Curt Tannahill.

She nodded and motioned for him to enter.

The policeman looked around the small room and at the three *kinder* huddled together on the sofa. Sympathy lengthened his face, but his expression became cool again as he turned to Beth Ann.

"Ms. Henderson has the right to a single phone call, but she's insisting she wants to speak with you in person, Ms. Overholt." He tugged at his heavy vest. "We don't usually make house calls in situations like this, but with you Amish not having phones, the chief thought this would be the simplest."

Robert wasn't surprised Beth Ann didn't correct his assumption she was Amish.

She began, "The children and I—"

"Just you, Ms. Overholt." His eyes shifted to the *kinder* and away. "You're the one she wants to see."

She nodded. "Robert, will you be okay staying with the children?"

He heard the question she didn't ask. Last time someone had wanted to speak to her alone, he'd been mad. But he'd been wrong about her meeting with the social worker alone, and he'd be even more wrong if he insisted on going with her to see Kim.

"Of course," he said, though he wanted to insist he go with her. "Let Kim know we're praying for her."

"Thank you," she whispered, and was gone.

Crystal and Tommy began crying again, and Dougie sniffled, trying not to sob, too. Sitting on the sofa, Robert held out his arms and offered them the silent comfort his *daed* had denied him. He hoped it would be enough.

Chapter Fifteen

Officer Tannahill gave Beth Ann a sympathetic look before motioning to follow him down a hallway. Dawn had arrived while she sat in the reception area, trying to be patient. Outside the one window she could see from her bench, the snow had thinned to the occasional flake, but various officers coming into the building had reported almost a foot had fallen.

Beth Ann wished Robert had been able to come with her. She longed to reach out and take his hand as she would have one of the children's. The comfort of someone familiar, someone who represented normalcy.

She wanted that connection to prove this wasn't an appalling nightmare.

Each door along the hall was shut, but she heard voices behind a few she passed. Someone laughed from a closed room, and she flinched. What could be funny in a place like this?

The officer, his thin face set in stern lines, looked to be about the same age as the children's mother. Had he gone through school with Kim Henderson?

"You can wait here, Ms. Overholt," he said with the slightest motion of his head toward a door to the left. Opening it, he pointed to a single table with two chairs. The room was otherwise bare. No calendar or window broke the institutional green color of the walls.

Beth Ann felt queasy. She wished Kim Henderson hadn't been so insistent the only person she'd talk to was Beth Ann.

Another door opened, and Kim walked in, wearing an ill-fitting jumpsuit and handcuffs. Seeing her in the bright light made Beth Ann realize how the woman resembled her children. She had the same bright red hair, though hers was mussed, and her face shared Crystal's delicate shape. Her eyes were like Dougie's had been when Beth Ann first met him on the village green. Filled with fear and anger. Dark circles surrounded them, and Beth Ann wondered when Kim had last slept.

A female officer led Kim to the table and latched her cuffs to it before stepping back. Neither she nor Officer Tannahill left the room.

"I hear," Kim said in lieu of greeting, "you've been taking care of my kids since that no-good sister of mine dumped them and headed to Vegas."

"I'm Beth Ann Overholt, and, yes, they've been staying with me."

"I hear you're rich." Her lips twisted in an impotent sneer. "Not that you dress like a rich woman. Where did you find that shapeless dress?"

Beth Ann ignored the question. "Where did you hear something like that?"

Kim shrugged. "I don't know. From a

bunch of people. Guess it's the talk of Evergreen Corners how some plain woman hit the lottery. I didn't know you Goody Two-shoes played the lottery."

"I don't."

"But you're loaded." She didn't make it a question.

"I'm not here to talk about me. I'm here to talk about your children."

"Are they okay?" The question created the first crack in Kim's hard demeanor, and Beth Ann felt sympathy stirring anew in her heart for the woman.

Knowing she must be honest, she said, "I hope they will be. It's not easy to see your mom arrested."

"It's not like it's the first time."

Beth Ann closed her eyes and sent a request heavenward for the right words to break through Kim's hard facade so they could talk.

"Why did you want to speak with me?" she asked.

Again Kim's gaze shifted away, but this

time to aim at the two officers. "Some privacy, okay?"

They moved to stand closer to the door where they could see, but when Kim lowered her voice, they couldn't overhear.

Kim folded her arms on the table, frowning as her handcuffs clattered. "Look. Here's the situation. I've got a deal for you."

"*You* have a deal for me?"

"Yeah. You take care of my problems, and I'll take care of yours."

"I don't understand."

Kim smiled. "It's simple. I need money for a good lawyer who'll get me out. One who'll let me plea for time served and won't insist I go to rehab."

"Weren't you getting help there?"

"What I was or wasn't getting isn't part of this discussion. What I want to talk about is making a deal so you pay for a lawyer who can promise me a get-out-of-jail-free card."

Beth Ann wasn't ready to agree to any such thing, but she couldn't keep from asking, "What would I get in return?"

"My kids."

"What?" She tried to say more, but words stuck in her throat. Kim was using her children to bargain for money?

Again Kim shrugged. "They can't be on their own. They're too little. I knew that when I got shipped off to rehab. My no-good sister didn't watch them like she promised, and I don't want my kids going into foster care. I grew up in the system, and I don't want my kids to."

"I agree."

"Good. So you'll help me?"

Her mind was so full of contradictory thoughts she couldn't think straight. "You want me to pay for a lawyer for you and in return I get to continue to watch the children. Is that right?"

"Not exactly. I want you to get me a lawyer who'll get the charges dropped and me out. You get my kids. I'll sign them over to you."

As her heart soared at the idea of having the children stay with her, Beth Ann exclaimed, "Kim, you can't mean that!"

Both cops turned toward them, but looked away when Kim scowled.

"I do." She wiped her nose with the back of her hand. "I'll sign away my rights. It's just me. Their fathers are dead."

"Fathers? I thought—"

"There were two, but I was foolish enough only to marry one." She eyed Beth Ann. "I hope I'm not shocking you."

Raising her chin, Beth Ann replied, "I may live plain, but I know how things happen."

"I'm sure you think you do." She leaned her elbow on the table and rested her chin on her hand. "You Amish?"

"No." She hadn't come to talk about herself. "Kim, your children need their mother."

"They need *a* mother, but not me. You seem like a nice lady. You'd make them a good mother." A faint smile slid along her lips. "I know you think I'm not worth much, but I'm good at figuring people out, and I figure you care a lot about my kids. Otherwise, why would you be here?"

"The children miss you."

"They'll get over it. I did when my mother dumped me and never came back."

Beth Ann understood. Kim didn't want her children moved from home to home, wondering if anyone in the world cared about them. She wasn't dumping Dougie, Crystal and Tommy because she loved her drugs more than she did them. She was seeking a way to give them a better future.

"I can't give you an answer today," Beth Ann said.

"My arraignment is Tuesday. It's taking that long because Christmas is on Saturday and Monday's a holiday. I'll need a lawyer. A good one. Not one of the public defenders just out of law school." She sniffed. "One of them got me stuck in rehab last time."

Beth Ann bit her lip to keep from saying the young public defender had done Kim a big favor. Infuriating the woman wouldn't help anyone.

When she remained silent, Kim asked, "Will you think about it?"

"I will."

"Get me an answer very, very soon."

"As soon as I can." Pushing back her chair, Beth Ann stood.

The two police officers moved toward the table. The woman unhooked Kim's cuffs from the table and led her away.

Beth Ann followed Officer Tannahill out. When he drove her back to Evergreen Corners and bid her to have a good day, she wondered if it was possible. Every cell within her was shaken by Kim's request to trade her children for a chance to continue her drug-addicted life.

When she opened the apartment door, she was astonished to see the living room filled with the friends she'd made in Evergreen Corners. The Whittakers, the Millers, the Kauffmans, Robert and his sister Rachel. Dougie, Crystal and Tommy regarded her with a mixture of hope and uncertainty.

She knelt in front of them. "Your mom looks okay, and she asked about you."

"Really?" Dougie wasn't as ready to swallow her statement as his siblings were.

"Yes." Glancing at her friends, she said,

"She talked about the three of you the whole time."

Abby stepped forward and held out her hands to the younger children. "*Komm* with me, and let's make those chocolate chip cookies I was telling you about."

Beth Ann said, "The social worker—"

"Is supposed to be here in about two hours, ain't so?" Abby's smile remained steady. "That will give me and the *kinder* plenty of time to have nice warm cookies ready."

"Can we go?" asked Crystal.

She thought Dougie might protest, but he got up along with his sister and brother. Pulling on their winter coats, they went with Abby out the door. Beth Ann could hear Tommy prattling about how his *penders* would make him a better baker.

Robert helped her draw off her coat. "How are you?"

She wished she could throw herself in his arms and sob as the children had in hers. It was impossible to tear the memory of Kim offering up her children from her memory.

Yet as she looked at the worried faces in the room, she knew she didn't have to deal with the problem by herself.

Not mincing words, she told them what Kim had asked of her. Worry became dismay and despair. When Isaac asked them to pray for the Henderson family, she bent her head. A sense of community, of belonging, of being where God meant her to be, filled her as she prayed.

Robert asked, "What can we do to help, Beth Ann?"

She guessed he had no idea how much that simple question gave her hope all wasn't lost. "I thought about it. I plan to ask Pastor Hershey and you, Gladys, to recommend a good lawyer for Kim."

"You'll pay for his or her services?"

"Yes."

"And you'll take the *kinder* in return?" Gladys asked. "You can't be thinking of doing that."

"Of course I'm not! The children aren't for sale. I've loved having them with me, but how would they feel if they discover what their mother had done?" She choked as she added, "What I'd done?"

Turning to the others, Robert cleared his throat. "I think Beth Ann and I need to talk."

Each person gave her a warm smile as he or she went out of the apartment. In their wake, silence fell on the room.

She dropped to the sofa and stared at the floor until Robert brought her a steaming cup.

"I thought you might want *kaffi*," he said.

"Thank you." She took a careful sip. It was stronger than she liked it, but she needed the boost of caffeine after a sleepless night.

As he sat facing her, he had her repeat the story again. He asked as soon as she was finished, "Are you going to tell Deana this?"

Ice clamped around her heart, so cold and deep she half expected the cup to freeze in her hand. "I hadn't thought about that. I know I should, but what if she takes the children away today?"

"She might not. If she doesn't have a placement for them—"

"I'm not ready to risk that. Are you?"

He stood. Not meeting her eyes, he said, "I don't think you should make me a part of any plan you're making for the *kinder.*"

"What?"

"I can't be part of it."

She recoiled, as shocked as if he'd slapped her. He'd been so calm, so steady, so much like that old bridge he wanted to repair. Battered around the edges, but refusing to collapse. Now he looked ill.

"What's wrong?" she asked. "You're not going to be part of *what*? The children's lives? You're already a part of those."

"I won't be much longer." He met her eyes. "I've been offered a job. A *gut* job."

She smiled. "Robert, that's great news! Congratulations!"

"It's in Rutland, more than an hour and a half away by car. I'll be moving there if I take the job."

Somehow she set the cup on the table

without dropping it. Everything she'd feared might happen was happening.

"Wouldn't you be able to come and visit on your days off?" she whispered.

"I could, but I shouldn't."

"I don't understand."

He met her puzzled gaze. "I know you don't, but I can't risk it."

"Risk what?"

"I almost lost my temper with Dougie the other night."

"And I did lose my temper with you. So what does that have to do with anything?"

He drew in a deep breath, then let it sift past his clenched teeth. "You losing your temper is different."

"How?"

"When you lost your temper, you yelled at me."

"That's what happens when I get angry. I'm not proud of it, but it's the way I am."

Squatting in front of her, he said, "You don't know me as well as you think you do. My *daed* was a cruel man, Beth Ann. I don't know why, but whenever he lost his temper or felt someone had insulted him or he had a bad day, he'd take it out on us, his *kinder*. Usually on Rachel, which is why she jumped the fence when she was seventeen. That was more than twenty years ago. I didn't see her again until a couple of months ago."

"Really?" She'd never guessed either Robert's or Rachel's past was filled with such pain and loss. "I'm so sorry."

"It's not something either of us talk about. Isaac knows, of course. He was set to defend Rachel and her daughters from *Daed*, if necessary, but it never was. *Daed* is dead, so he can't beat us ever again."

"Your father beat you?"

He nodded. "*Ja*. More than once we should have gone to the hospital, but he refused to take us. His legacies are a load of debt and a temper that could destroy me and anyone near to me."

She cupped his face. "You don't have to be like your father. You say I don't know you, but I do. You're kind and loving."

"You don't know what I'm like inside. My *daed*'s temper—"

A fist hammered on the door, and Isaac burst into the apartment. "Robert, the Hendersons' house is collapsing. Last night's snowstorm must have been too much for the roof."

Jumping to her feet, she said, "Go, Robert!"

"You, too, Beth Ann."

"I've got the social worker coming in—"

Isaac snapped, "You need to *komm*! Dougie is in the house!"

Robert wondered if his face was as colorless as Beth Ann's. They ran after Isaac through snow that reached over the top of his boots to the Hendersons' street. The sound of sirens came from every direction. As they raced around the corner, he saw both a fire truck and an ambulance coming up from the center of the village. Police cars were speeding toward them from higher up the hill.

As he watched, the house slid another few

inches backwards, and the tub fell through the porch. The crowd in front of the house yelled warnings. Either the foundation had failed or a joist supporting the house had broken. He pushed toward the house where Abby was trying to get Tommy and Crystal out of the way.

A sharp creak came from above them, and shingles pelted the street. He grabbed Beth Ann with one hand and the *kinder* with the other. Abby scurried away with them.

Shouts followed the sound of glass cracking in the windows and falling to the porch. The supports for the porch roof teetered.

Robert whirled to the *kinder.* "Are you sure he's in there?"

Crystal nodded, tears flooding her cheeks.

"Beth Ann, stay with the kids."

"Where are you going?"

"To get Dougie, of course."

"What if the house collapses?"

He grasped her shoulders. "I know my

way around tumbledown structures. Remember? I was going to fix the old bridge."

"I don't want to lose both of you."

"You aren't going to lose either of us." He pulled her close for a swift kiss, not caring that people saw. It was more difficult than he'd guessed to end it.

As he released her, she whispered, "Get Dougie and get out fast!"

He touched her cheek with two fingers before running to the house. A shout came from behind him as he climbed the tilting steps. He saw a police officer waving him away from the house.

Instead he rushed inside. The floors were sloping at a precarious angle. He lurched forward, using the tilting banister to pull himself along. His name was shouted, and he looked back to see a policeman in the doorway.

"I'm getting Dougie Henderson," he called back.

"Let me help. Do you know where he might be?"

"I don't—" The floor quaked under his

feet, and he grasped the railing with both hands.

The policeman seized the door molding before it cracked and fell off the wall. It missed Robert by inches. Dust flew up to smother them.

Through the noise of dishes shattering, Robert heard his name. Not from outside, but from the dining room.

"This way." He pushed away from the stairs.

The table was upside down by the far wall. Plaster covered it, but his eyes fixed on an arm waving above it.

Moving as quickly as he could, he rounded the end of the table. Relief exploded within him when he saw Dougie pressed to the wall. He bent to embrace the boy, then noticed his right leg was at a strange angle beneath the table. Against his chest, Dougie held a dirty sock, and tears coursed down his face.

Robert shouted to the policeman to alert the EMTs and bent to lift the table off the boy's leg. When he realized Dougie couldn't move his leg by himself, Robert hefted the table toward the rear of the house. It crashed into the kitchen wall, sending more dust and plaster down on them.

He slipped his arms under the boy. Scrambling to his feet, he staggered across the floor. The boards beneath his feet seemed more like a trampoline than solid lumber. More creaks came from around them.

"We've got to get out," Dougie said.

Robert took one step forward, and the house shifted. Cracks climbed the wall. Plaster dust blinded him.

A hand grasped his elbow. He recognized the slender fingers and wanted to shout at Beth Ann to get out of the house. He couldn't talk because he could hardly breathe.

Someone seized his other arm, pulling him up the ever-steeper floor. He stumbled through the door. Beth Ann's arm went around him after Dougie was plucked from his hold. She pushed him off the porch.

Behind them a loud crash sent a gray cloud billowing through the broken windows. He coughed, struggling to breathe. Did he hear someone say the rear of the house had fallen in? He wasn't sure.

"Are you okay?" Beth Ann asked as her arm propped him up again.

"*Ja*. Dougie?"

"There." She led him to where the boy was being placed on a gurney. A woman was already examining his right leg and called for splints to stabilize it.

Robert straightened. How could Dougie have been so careless? He looked from the sock the boy clutched to his face. The fright there quelled Robert's fury.

"Are you going to punish me?" the boy asked in a small voice.

"*Ja*."

He stiffened. "You'll have to catch me to spank me."

"Catching you won't be hard when you've broken your leg, but I'm not going to spank you."

Disbelief filled Dougie's voice. "I deserve it."

"*Ja*, you do, but I'm not going to spank

you. You know what you did was wrong, ain't so?"

"I guess so."

"You *guess* so?"

"Yeah." He looked past Robert.

Beth Ann and the younger *kinder* edged closer. The EMT assured her that except for Dougie's leg, he was fine.

"Why?" Beth Ann said as she took the boy's hand. "Why did you go in there when you knew the house was condemned?"

"I had to get Mommy's money."

"You went in there for money?" Disbelief filled Beth Ann's voice. "How could you be so foolish when you know I've got enough money for whatever you need?"

"I didn't want to ask you."

She blinked as abrupt tears rushed into her eyes. "Because you wanted the money to help your mother?"

"No!" He gave her the way-too-familiar frown that suggested she didn't have a brain in her head. Looking at Robert, he asked, "You understand, don't you?"

She was astonished when Robert replied, "*Ja*, I do."

"Then one of you explain it to me!" she pleaded.

"It's simple, Beth Ann." He faced her. "He didn't go in there to get the money for Kim. He went in to get it so she couldn't get her hands on it."

Dougie nodded.

Comprehension was a clap of thunder resonating through Beth Ann. Dougie didn't want his mother to take the easy way out by abusing more drugs. He wanted her to get the help she needed. In spite of the times she'd abandoned him and his siblings, he loved his mother.

"*What* is going on?" demanded a woman from behind her.

Beth Ann wanted to groan when she heard Deana's question. Knowing she had to give the social worker a quick and honest answer, she wondered if there was any way to salvage the situation.

Gladys appeared out of the crowd. "You're the children's social worker, aren't you? Come with me, young lady, and I'll explain everything to you." She steered Deana away before the social worker could ask a single question.

"Our social worker?" asked Crystal. "Why is she here?"

"Is she taking us away?" Dougie winced as he spoke.

"Take us away?" Tommy began to cry. "No, no, no!"

"We want to live with you, Beth Ann," Crystal said with the passion of an eight-year-old who saw no shades of gray. "Don't send us away. Please, don't."

"I never would send you away, but—"

The EMT said, "I'm sorry to interrupt, but we need to get Dougie to the hospital to have X-rays."

"Can I go with him?" Beth Ann pleaded.

"Yes, but only one parent can ride in the ambulance."

Robert curved his hand along her cheek. "Go! After you get home, we need to talk."

"I know." As she was handed up into the vehicle and shown where to sit beside the gurney, she couldn't pull her gaze away from Robert's until the door closed. Folding Dougie's hand between hers, she forced herself to focus on the present. She had no idea what the future would bring, but feared it wouldn't include either Robert or the children.

Tony Whittaker brought Beth Ann and Dougie back on freshly plowed roads to Evergreen Corners as the sun set beyond the Green Mountains. The mayor's husband helped her tote the boy up the stairs after a single glance revealed Robert wasn't steady on his feet. Dried blood on his hair marked where debris had glanced off his head, but he'd already taken a couple of ibuprofen and felt better.

Abby sent supper, and Dougie was asleep before dessert was over. Beth Ann shared in furtive whispers what Dougie had told her at the hospital. The sock, which now contained less than thirty dollars, had been the way Dougie had paid for most of the groceries to be delivered to the apartment. He'd used a computer in the school library to place the order and then hidden the money for the deliveryman. That explained why, once the children were home-schooled, the deliveries halted.

Beth Ann tucked each child in with Robert's help. She'd expected them to be wired because they'd have presents in the morning, but the day had left them exhausted. Soon they all were asleep.

She cleared the table and washed the dishes, telling Robert to sit so she didn't have to worry about him falling. That he complied told her his head must have been aching more than she'd guessed.

As she wrung the dishrag, he said, "We never finished our conversation earlier."

"No, but I've had plenty of time to think about what you said." She faced him and leaned against the counter. "If the job in Rutland is a good one, you need to take it, Robert. The children will be gone in a couple of weeks, so there's no reason for you to stay."

"Do you think the children are the only consideration?"

"No, but you need to think about your future."

"My future shouldn't include *kinder*."

His words, spoken with regret, shocked her. "You're great with the kids. If you're talking about your temper, when have you lost it with them?"

"I almost lost it today and the other night I almost—"

"Listen to yourself, Robert! *I almost lost it*. But you didn't. You controlled your temper."

"Barely."

"Don't you see? God doesn't ask us to do anything but our best, and you've done your best to keep your temper in check."

"I might not always be able to control it."

"You aren't your father. You know the pain and degradation of abuse." She sat beside him. "You and Rachel are both wonderful with children." Stroking his cheek, she said, "Take the job. We'll figure out the future one day at a time."

"So you've decided what you want?"

"Yes, I want what I have here. A place where I can feel as if I belong with people who care about me and whom I care about. I came to Evergreen Corners because I thought I'd have a chance to think about what I wanted, but I've come to realize I've got everything I want and everything I need." She took a deep breath. "I'll use the money my aunt left me to buy Mrs. Weiskopf's store and a home in Evergreen Corners. I plan to fight to keep the children and to talk to Isaac about being baptized Amish."

"What?" His eyes became as round as a cereal bowl. "You'd have to give up your car and your phone and—"

"It's not about what I'd give up. It's what I'd gain. A loving faith family and a community where I know I belong." She raised her gaze to meet his and whispered, "And a chance to be with the man I love."

"You love me?"

She laughed. "Of course I do, you silly

man! I don't go around kissing random guys."

When he dropped to his knees beside her and clasped her hands in his, he said, "I love you, too, but I suspect you already know because you seem to know everything I'm thinking."

"I've *prayed* that you loved me." She leaned her forehead against his. "I asked God to put me on the path He wanted me to walk, and He brought me to you."

Muted giggles came from the doorway. She saw the three children, Dougie propped up by his sister and brother, grinning at them.

Her face was tilted toward Robert's as he said, "Let's give our eavesdroppers something worth listening to. Beth Ann, will you have an unemployed, broke Amish man for your husband?"

"I can't think of anyone I'd rather marry." As he stood, drawing her to her feet and into his arms, he bent to kiss her. The joyful dance of her heart matched the children's cheers.

Epilogue

How fast a year passed when surrounded by loving family and friends! As Beth Ann packed what she'd need at her sister-in-law's house for Christmas Day, she edged past the excited *kinder* in their comfortable house at the edge of the village. It wasn't far from where the other Amish families lived and close enough so she could walk to the general store. The store that she bought with her inheritance, the store that made her happy because she could stay in Evergreen Corners and had found a way still to help others.

Dougie rushed past her to grab his black hat. He seemed to grow another inch every day, and he was the first to brag about the kitchen skills she'd gained in the past year, though she and Robert reminded him that boasting wasn't acceptable for a plain family. Dougie just gave them one of his grins. One day, he'd challenge Robert's height, and Beth Ann had to let down the hems on his trousers almost every week. His little brother, celebrating his sixth birthday today, was a scholar at the new Amish school along with the older two. Tommy had mastered *Deitsch* more quickly than his siblings, a fact he never let them forget.

"Don't forget these, *Mamm*," said Crystal as she handed Beth Ann three bottles for the *boppli* who was asleep in the basket on the sofa.

"Danki, liebling." She thanked the Lord for the three older *kinder* who were as dear to her as little Lena.

Since Lena had arrived more than a month early the week before Thanksgiving, Beth Ann had split her time between home and the hospital. Finally, last week, the *boppli* had been released to come home.

Even before Beth Ann and Robert had married as soon as she was baptized, they'd worked with DCF to keep Dougie, Crystal and Tommy.

First, there had been the paperwork signed by Kim, after she returned to rehab and stayed there long enough to get clean, to give up custody of her *kinder*. Her sister had remained in Las Vegas where she'd found a *gut* job and was trying to convince Kim to join her far away from the environment that had led to her addiction.

With the *kinder* available for adoption, Beth Ann and Robert had arranged for a home study. The same week it'd been finished, she'd discovered they were going to have a *boppli*.

Two days after Lena's arrival, the adoption paperwork had been signed and Dougie, Crystal and Tommy became Yoders, happily embracing a plain life. Her family—her Amish family—was her dream come true.

"All set?" Robert picked up the basket with little Lena. His steps were the light ones of a man who had everything he wanted in his life.

In the past year, he'd learned it was okay to get angry, because he was in charge of his feelings, not the other way around. It was also okay to be happy, which he'd had more trouble accepting. That had turned around when the purchase of the general store was completed, and Beth Ann showed him the storeroom where he could have his woodworking shop.

He hadn't been able to start right away, because he'd been hired to supervise the rebuilding of the covered bridge once Gladys procured the special funding she'd sought. In October, on the second anniversary of the devastating flood, the first cars had driven across it. The following day, Yoder's Woodworking hung out its shingle on the store's porch. Robert had, through his hard work and amazing skills, earned enough to pay off the last of his *daed*'s debts.

"We're set," Beth Ann said, motioning for the *kinder* to head out the door and get in the buggy for the short journey to their *aenti*'s and *onkel*'s house. She couldn't wait to see the *kinder*'s faces when they discovered that Kim, now free of drugs and living in a halfway house, was joining them for supper.

"Merry Christmas," he murmured before he kissed her. "The happiest one yet."

"Ja." She slipped her hand onto his arm. "Because I have received the greatest gifts anyone could want. My family and my husband and my *wunderbaar* home and friends."

"Just what you wanted?"

"Ja."

He tapped her nose as if she were no older than Crystal. "Me, too."

* * * * *

If you enjoyed this story,
don't miss these other books
from Jo Ann Brown:

The Amish Suitor
The Amish Christmas Cowboy
The Amish Bachelor's Baby
The Amish Widower's Twins
An Amish Christmas Promise
An Amish Easter Wish
An Amish Mother's Secret Past

Find more great reads at
www.LoveInspired.com

Dear Reader,

Isn't it interesting that when we're not sure what we're supposed to do next in our lives, the answer can be unexpected? As I neared the end of college, unsure what I wanted to do next, being commissioned as an officer in the US Army wasn't on my radar, but when the opportunity came, I took it. Finding which door God will open for us next is exciting, isn't it?

The Mennonite Disaster Service is a real organization established seventy years ago. MDS volunteers come from the US and Canada and have helped rebuild homes and lives after disasters, usually weather-related or due to wildfires.

Visit me at www.joannbrownbooks.com. This is the final book in Evergreen Corners, Vermont. I hope you've enjoyed your visit. My next series will be set in the new Amish community on Prince Edward Island.

Wishing you many blessings,
Jo Ann Brown